WORMS OF ENDEARMENT

A PARANORMAL MYSTERY ADVENTURE

MONSTERS OF JELLYFISH BEACH 7

WARD PARKER

wardparker.com

CONTENTS

CHAPTER 1
TOXIC RELATIONSHIP

"Milo is more passionate about the Mongolian Death Worm than about me," said the wife of the famous cryptozoologist. "And he never even laid eyes on the stupid worm."

Ah, romance, I thought as Claire Fusseldink frowned with resentment of her husband, who had gone missing during an expedition to Mongolia.

As a member of the Friends of Cryptids Society, I would be expected to empathize with Milo's passion. The "stupid worm" was a crown jewel of cryptozoology, one of the most coveted legendary creatures sought by humankind and almost as famous as Bigfoot himself. Yet a desert-dwelling creature that spat venom at its victims was not appealing to me, no matter how hard I tried to care about it. The only reason I was visiting the Fusseldink home was to provide my services as a witch.

"How long has he been missing?" I asked from a chair facing the couch where she sat.

"Over three weeks—twenty-four days to be exact. He disappeared shortly after the expedition arrived in the Gobi Desert. He allegedly went hunting for the worm alone at night and was never seen again." The woman's jet-black eyebrows undulated in disbelief, almost worm-like. She was attractive and younger than I'd expect for the wife of the scientist who was in his sixties. Behind her was a window facing the Atlantic Ocean. These were awfully nice digs for a pseudo-scientist, unless his wife was the one who brought home the bacon.

"I'm sorry," I mumbled. "I hope my spell will help locate him."

"Can you believe the expedition has returned to the States already? Such a disgrace! What kind of colleagues are they to abandon Milo so quickly?"

"They must have run out of provisions," I suggested. "It can't be easy to camp in the Gobi Desert."

"Someone should have stayed in Mongolia until Milo was found to ensure the locals keep searching for him. Jude Levings, the co-leader, for instance. It's the least I would expect." Claire was driving herself into a rage.

"Shall we begin the spell-casting process?" I asked, eager to divert her mood. My witchy help had been promised to her by Mrs. Lupis and Mr. Lopez, my handlers at the Friends of Cryptids Society. I'd never attempted to use my locator spell to find someone on the other side of the planet and was anxious about whether it would work.

"Yes. Let's get on with it. What do you need from me, Missy?"

"A possession that your husband loves and regularly handles, because it will be filled with his spiritual energy. It could be a golf club, a favorite hat, the TV remote, or something similar. Does that make sense?"

"Milo didn't have hobbies; he was so devoted to his work. I have a couple of boxes of his notebooks and photos that were sent back from Mongolia, but I wouldn't know where to start."

"Do you have any of his DNA, like shed hair?"

"I do. On his hairbrush!" She smiled at me, triumphant. "Not only will that have his hair on it, but he was rather a narcissist, and he'd gaze lovingly in the mirror when he brushed his hair. It should have lots of his spiritual energy."

"That sounds very promising."

"His main brush should still be in his dresser. He took a smaller, travel brush to Mongolia." She got up from the couch and disappeared down a hallway leading to the bedrooms.

Seconds later, an ear-splitting shriek came from that direction, followed by the slam of a body landing upon hardwood flooring.

I rushed into the hallway, running past closed rooms toward the open door of the master bedroom. It faced the ocean and was a bright, cheery room except for one detail: Claire Fusseldink lay face-up on the floor in front of a dresser with an open drawer. She was unconscious.

Her facial expression, however, was bright and cheery. With closed eyes and a huge grin, she looked blissed out as if she'd had a massage. Belying her expression were yellow splotches on her face and neck and, not the least of which, that she didn't appear to be breathing.

I knelt beside her and placed my fingers on her neck, feeling for the carotid artery. No pulse.

The 911 operator asked me if I was certain the victim was dead and what the cause was.

"Yes, I am certain," I replied. "And I have no idea what happened."

I glanced inside the open top drawer of the dresser. It was full of dress socks with the handle of a wooden hairbrush visible. A strange odor came from inside: hints of cinnamon mixed with an unpleasant, acrid scent. A deep instinct told me not to touch anything, not just to avoid disturbing any evidence, but because it felt dangerous to do so.

Pacing around the room, I kept my eyes on Mrs. Fusseldink, searching my memory for knowledge from my previous nursing career for a likely cause of death. I believed the only logical explanations were an unusual type of stroke or a toxin of some sort.

Then I heard it: a slithering sound beneath the dresser. I jumped away from it and peered into the dark, shallow space created by the furniture's squat legs. What was under there?

The scuffling, slithering sound now came from under a club chair near the window. Was there more than one creature, or was it simply adept at moving quickly and unseen?

I glanced back at Mrs. Fusseldink's mottled face with its goofy grin and wondered the impossible: could she have been killed by a Mongolian death worm?

No way, I thought. No specimen of the legendary creature had ever been found. Mrs. Fusseldink's husband traveled to the other side of the planet to search for the darned thing and went missing instead. Mrs. Lupis and Mr. Lopez hadn't said anything about the expedition achieving success.

The searchers returned to the US, though. Perhaps they hadn't come empty-handed.

"If it's a death worm, we must capture it." I jumped at the familiar voice.

My two handlers, clad in their perennial gray suits, stood just outside the bedroom doorway. I didn't even bother to ask how and why they showed up just now.

"Did you see it?" Mr. Lopez asked me.

"No. I only heard something slithering around. It might be a snake, for all I know."

"Or the Mongolian Death Worm," he said. "My word, look at what happened to her face. Why is she smiling?"

"We must capture the worm," Mrs. Lupis repeated.

"How exactly?" I asked. "Legend says the worm spits venom, and look at what happened to the victim's face. How are we supposed to grab it without ending up dead like her?"

"We were hoping the Fusseldink expedition would have solved that and returned with a specimen in a box," Mr. Lopez said.

I stepped on top of an ottoman so my feet would be less vulnerable. "If the Mongolian Death Worm is in this room, someone from the expedition put it here. To kill Mrs. Fusseldink, I guess."

"This is not the time to specu—watch out!" Mrs. Lupis shrieked, leaping away from the doorway as a rapid sliding sound came from the open closet door nearby.

"Is there a fishing net in this house?" asked Mr. Lopez from far down the hallway where he had escaped.

"I doubt it," I replied. "I got the impression that there were no hobbies or recreation for this family. Except cryptid research."

Mr. Lopez shrieked at a pitch higher even than Mrs. Lupis. "It's in the living room!"

The crackling of a radio came from the front of the house, and the front door opened.

"Hello? Police," called a female voice.

"Come in," I shouted. "The body is back here."

Officer Bird, a young cop I recognized from my frequent presence at crime scenes, entered the master bedroom, followed by two male paramedics. "Oh, hi Missy. Why is everyone standing on furniture?"

"Trying not to contaminate the crime scene," I lied.

"Who says it's a crime scene?"

"Well, it's not a slip-and-fall accident. The victim appears to have been—"

A loud cough came from Mrs. Lupis, who was standing on a small table in the hall. She swung her fingertips across her throat in a "cut it off" gesture.

"We don't know what the cause of death was," she said to Bird.

"I think she was exposed to a toxin," one of the paramedics said. "Why is she smiling?"

"Could *we* be harmed by the toxin?" Bird asked as she tried the handles of the French doors leading to an oceanfront balcony.

"Possibly. Don't touch anything." The paramedic and his partner jogged out of the room and left the house.

The officer turned pale and inched her way out of the bedroom. "The balcony doors are unlocked, meaning someone could have escaped before Missy entered the room. If there's any possibility this is a homicide, I need to get a detective here."

She murmured something into her radio, including the street address.

"Did the paramedics close the front door behind them?" I asked her.

"Nope."

I remained quiet, listening for rustling or slithering sounds. There were none. I worried that the death worm—assuming that was what it was—had escaped from the house.

The paramedics came back inside and returned to the bedroom, wheeling a gurney. They now wore full hazmat suits but had brought none to share with us. *Gee, thanks for thinking of our safety, too.*

"Did you see any sort of creature escaping the house?" I asked.

The paramedics answered with muffled noes as they placed Mrs. Fusseldink in a body bag, zipping it shut with finality.

I assumed it was safe to step down from the ottoman, and I headed for the living room. Mrs. Lupis and Mr. Lopez eventually summoned the courage to leave their perches and followed me there.

Before we could talk strategy, Detective Cindy Shortle arrived and approached us. "I need statements from all of you."

My handlers convinced her they had arrived post-mortem and had come here to interview Mrs. Fusseldink about her famous cryptozoologist husband. I concocted a story about serving as a medium who was going to attempt to contact Milo's spirit to find out if he was dead. The rest of the story, about Claire stepping into the bedroom and dying, was true. I merely left out the parts about my magic spell and the slithering sounds.

Shortle gave me a piercing stare, her hair pulled so tight in a ponytail that it made her eyes look more severe. "This death didn't have anything to do with witchcraft, did it?"

"As I've told you many times before, I'm not an actual witch," I said with as much of a tone of innocence as I could muster. "Just a magic hobbyist. And a medium. Besides, why would I want to harm Mrs. Fusseldink? I'd only just met her."

"What about your mother, the black-magic practitioner operating in Jellyfish Beach?"

"I wouldn't know." It hadn't occurred to me that my mother could be connected to this murder. I couldn't think of a reason why.

"If the surveillance cameras show that you're the only person visiting the house today," Shortle warned, "don't get too cocky. Or you'll end up as a suspect."

I thought about taking the hairbrush, but Shortle ushered us out of the house. She put crime-scene tape across the door should the autopsy warrant further investigation. The young detective left my handlers and me standing on the sloped driveway of the oceanfront home.

"Excuse me," a woman called from the driveway next door. "Was there a burglary at the Fusseldinks' home?"

"You could say it was a bit more serious than that," I replied.

"I've seen police cars here before. Claire said it was because of burglaries. There are so many more cars this time."

Mrs. Lupis and Mr. Lopez glared at me, warning me to shut

up, and herded me down the driveway away from the neighbor. I had been about to blab the truth about Mrs. Fusseldink, but it was probably for the best that I hadn't.

"The Society must keep a low profile around crime scenes," Mr. Lopez explained. "That includes you, too."

Trying to change the subject, I mentioned my observation that the home seemed out of the realm of affordability for a cryptozoologist. "Was Claire a doctor, lawyer, or CEO?"

"Mrs. Fusseldink was a corporate attorney. Plus, she came from money," Mrs. Lupis replied.

"Big money," her partner added.

"That could be an incentive for Milo to kill her."

The two looked at me as if I'd farted in church. "Milo Fusseldink is our hero," they said simultaneously.

"Perhaps the most famous cryptozoologist of all time," added Mrs. Lupis.

"*Human* cryptozoologist," her partner clarified.

I studied their faces: hers was Caucasian; his had light-brown skin. Both had jet-black hair. And neither was human. What exactly they were, I did not know.

"Even famous scientists commit murders now and then," I said.

They continued to give me that horrified look.

"Okay," I admitted. "Maybe my theory was a stretch. After all, why would someone put the worm in Milo's dresser drawer if it was meant to kill *her*?"

"The worm could have been placed anywhere, and it ended up in that drawer," Mr. Lopez said. "You saw how easily the thing moved around the house."

"And it did so unseen, too," Mrs. Lupis said.

"Which is why we don't know for sure it was the Mongolian Death Worm," I reminded them. "Could've been a snake. Or a scorpion. A lizard. It could have been just a random critter that got inside the house and had nothing to do with killing Mrs. Fusseldink. A human might have poisoned her in some fashion."

"It would be too much of a coincidence if she was killed by anything other than the 'random critter' we heard."

"We have a hunch it's the death worm. And when we have hunches," said Mr. Lopez, "they're usually correct."

"Regardless, we need to find out who is behind this and why," I said. "The death worm didn't travel by itself from Mongolia. Someone brought it to the US and put it in the Fusseldinks' home. That's what we need the authorities to focus on. Not the creature that created the toxin. We don't want to risk allowing a rare cryptid to get killed by the police or Animal Control."

"I agree," said Mr. Lopez. "Mrs. Fusseldink's death will hopefully be blamed on an evil human, not a cryptid behaving according to its nature. We must protect the creature while punishing the perpetrator."

"Punish?"

"Of course. As you well know, the Friends of Cryptids Society doesn't just study and protect the many species of monsters. We also ensure they don't create problems with the human population. Creatures that kill humans must be removed from society—moved elsewhere, held in captivity at the Cryptid Sanctuary, or euthanized."

"Right. As *you* well know, I've assisted our enforcer, Angela, many times. But the death worm was only being itself when it killed Mrs. Fusseldink. Why would you punish it? We only need to capture and study it."

"I meant punish the human murderer who brought the worm to this house, before they're punished by the regular justice system."

"The Society isn't law enforcement."

"We have our own justice department," Mrs. Lupis said. "Humans who use cryptids to harm others violate our laws in addition to human laws."

"We have laws? I thought we just have annoying rules and regulations."

"Cryptids and other monsters essentially have their own community. We're responsible for enforcing its laws."

This conversation was disturbing me. "What would the punishment be for a human who committed murder-by-worm?"

Mr. Lopez shrugged. "This is such a rare crime that we don't know what the punishment would be. First, the mystery must be solved, and the murderer must be caught. That's where you come in, Ms. Mindle."

"Me?"

"Yes. You are our witch-detective, and we have tremendous faith in your ability to find and take down the murderer."

"If I'm not taken down first." I said it sarcastically but should have known my words would be prophetic.

CHAPTER 2
SWAMPLAND U

Matt kissed me lightly before sitting across from me at the outdoor cafe, our beachfront go-to meeting place. It was a beautiful, sunny morning with a calm sea and joggers streaming by on the sidewalk. My newspaper-reporter friend and partner in crime solving poured himself a cup of coffee from the carafe and glanced at the breakfast menu.

"Well?" I asked.

"I'll probably get the usual egg platter."

"No, 'well' was an inquiry about the autopsy report."

"Shortle promised she'll let me know when she gets it. Sometimes the medical examiner is backed up, and they can't get to it right away." He sipped his coffee. "And you know that toxicology reports could take even longer. The initial speculation is that the victim was sprayed with some sort of acid, based on the burns on her face. It doesn't seem like it would kill her, though."

"Or make her smile with bliss."

"True. Anyway, there's nothing we can do but wait."

"Oh, yes, there's plenty we can do. Like investigate the expedition party. Mrs. Fusseldink said they've returned from Mongolia, even though Milo is still missing."

"They abandoned their leader?"

"Actually, he was more of a co-leader. Professor Jude Levings from Swampland University was his partner. Milo was the famous one; Levings was the one who got funding from his university for the expedition. I spent hours scouring the internet last night."

"Tell me what you know," Matt asked, a spark of intrigue in his eyes.

"The *allghoi khorkhoi*, or Mongolian Death Worm, is a creature that has fascinated cryptozoologists since before there was a name for their field. The worm has been part of the folklore of the nomads from the northern and southern Gobi Desert for centuries, though no specimens have ever been found. But the locals claim that a relative of a friend of a friend has seen one—you know how it goes. Supposedly, the worms burrow beneath the sand and occasionally emerge onto the surface, spitting venom on their prey. They can also shock you with electricity. One legend tells of an entire herd of camels killed by worms."

"Why would anyone want to capture one of these?"

"I don't know. Bragging rights? Anyway, there have been many expeditions by Westerners searching for the worm since the twentieth century. On one of them, they used a machine to pound the sand, hoping the rhythmic thumping would draw worms to the surface."

"Ah, sort of like in *Dune*." Matt smiled.

"Or the worm grunters."

"The what?"

"You've never heard of the Worm Gruntin' Festival in Sopchoppy, up in the Florida Panhandle?"

He shook his head.

"You're the fisherman, not me. It's an old-fashioned way of gathering earthworms for bait. The locals pound wooden stakes into the ground and then rub them with flat pieces of metal. The vibrations make the worms think moles are burrowing for them, so they escape to the surface."

Matt stroked his beard in thought. "And that really works?"

"With earthworms. Apparently, not with death worms. From what I've read, the death worms probably aren't really worms but are actually reptiles. Anyway, the Fusseldink-Levings Expedition used the same vibration techniques, along with infrared cameras to monitor the desert at night. They spent three weeks covering hundreds of miles of territory and interviewing dozens of locals but came up empty."

"When did Fusseldink disappear?"

"At the beginning of the trip. He supposedly left his tent to check on the cameras one night and was never seen again."

"And the rest of the party just went home without him?"

"Yep. Their search came up empty-handed, and their funding ran out. I also read that there was bad blood between Fusseldink and Levings. So, the team simply left word about the disappearance with local authorities and the American consulate before heading home."

"Okay. So, what's your theory of how the worm ended up in the Fusseldink's bedroom?"

"The simplest explanation," I said, "is that the expedition

actually did find a worm, and someone put it in the bedroom to kill Claire."

"Or to kill Dr. Fusseldink."

"Nah."

He pushed back. "How can you be sure?"

"Everyone knows Milo is missing in Mongolia."

"Then, who would want to kill Claire?"

"That's what we need to find out."

"We? You want to rope me into yet another crazy Missy adventure? I thought this breakfast was simply for us to catch up."

"You know me better than that. I can't turn away from a murder."

"What do the Friends of Cryptids Society say?"

"They want me to find and capture the worm. That sounds impossible. I think we'll have better luck finding out who did this. If the police or civilians don't find the worm first."

"What if it kills someone else?"

"Unlikely," I said, probably jinxing it.

"This isn't the Gobi Desert. This is a small city. Jellyfish Beach has a lot of residents who would be at risk."

I signaled to the server to take our orders. "There's no sense in debating this further. Let's learn more about the expedition."

Professor Jude Levings taught cryptozoology and conspiracy theory at Swampland University in South Florida, at the edge of the Everglades. He was the Swamp Ape Fellow at the institution, one of the few in the world where students could blow their parents' money on such arcane educational topics. Matt and I each attempted to reach him via the university, and through Levings's official and private phone, email, and social media.

He steadfastly refused to answer us. However, the university helpfully referred us to a graduate research assistant of his. She was distrusting of Matt because he was a reporter, but my affiliation with the Friends of Cryptids Society won her over, and she agreed to meet. Matt and I made the drive in my car along Alligator Alley, the interstate highway that crossed the Everglades, to the small town near Fort Myers that was home to the university.

Zora Marchovsky met us at a bookstore cafe. She was a petite dyed-blonde, with a loud Eastern-European accent that belied her small stature.

"Do you believe in the existence of the Mongolian Death Worm?" was how she greeted us, as if demanding a password for entrance to a secret society. She bellowed her question with no concern for the customers hearing her. But they paid her no attention. Weird talk probably happened all the time in a town full of students studying cryptozoology.

"Yes," Matt and I answered simultaneously. Doing so made us sound like my Society handlers, which was kind of weird.

While Matt went to the counter to get our beverages, I sat at the table and told her earnestly, "I believe strongly in the creature."

Zora smiled. "I find that reassuring after all we've been through."

"Did your expedition find any evidence at all?"

"We found tracks in the sand leading from a hole in the ground, as well as a small amount of spoor. It was impossible to determine if they were from a worm, but we suspected they were. It was more than previous expeditions had found."

"Any other evidence?"

She smiled bitterly. "Yes. We found a molted skin. We're certain it was shed by a death worm. Unfortunately."

"Why, 'unfortunately'?"

"The skin went missing. We believe Milo Fusseldink took it before he disappeared."

"Overall, do you consider the expedition somewhat of a success?"

"Without the skin, you could say it was an enormous waste of time."

"Do you know anything about the venom the worm allegedly spits?"

"We interviewed several villagers and desert nomads. Some claim they had heard indirectly of animals and the rare person killed by the worms. They say the venom is like an acid, damaging flesh and blinding eyes, and it kills quickly. Except in one strange case."

"Tell me," I implored.

"Many years ago, a goat herder was sprayed, but only partially. He suffered some burns, but his eyes were not damaged. Strangely, he reported euphoric feelings. He said it was like smoking opium, but more intense. Odd, isn't it?"

This, finally, caused people overhearing her at nearby tables to look at Zora.

"What's this about opium?" Matt asked, delivering two coffees and my tea to the table.

I repeated what Zora had told me.

"Fascinating," he said as he sat down and slurped his coffee. "What evolutionary reason would there be for a toxin to cause pleasure?"

"If it is true," Zora said, "it could help the worm kill and eat prey. If the prey didn't receive enough venom, it would escape in pain. But if it experienced an intense pleasure that was stronger than the burn pain, the prey might allow the worm to squirt it again and kill it."

"You said the worms eat the prey?" I asked.

"Of course. That's what venomous snakes do."

"Rattlesnakes and cobras don't eat people."

"If you lived in a desert, you would eat whatever you could to survive."

"The Mongolian Death Worm is even scarier than I'd thought." Matt shook his head in disbelief.

"Incidences of humans being consumed were very, very rare," Zora said. "However, when carcasses of animals or humans are found in the desert, they have usually been partially consumed by scavengers. No one would know if a worm had done it."

After that lovely thought, we silently drank our beverages. Until I changed the subject.

"What is your theory about what happened to Dr. Fusseldink?"

Zora tensed up. "I don't have a clue."

"I understand there's bad blood between him and Professor Levings. Do you think—"

"Don't you dare imply that Professor Levings had anything to do with the disappearance."

"I'm not," I said in a soothing voice, hoping to calm her down. I briefly considered using my truth-telling spell on her, but my ethics forbade its use except on people I strongly suspected of being perpetrators of crimes and those who were obviously lying. Zora appeared to be neither.

There would be no harm in casting a calming spell, though. Not just for Zora, but for me, too. After activating the quick, simple spell, I sensed relaxation in all of us, even Matt, who was almost always wound too tight.

"Did Dr. Fusseldink and Professor Levings argue over control of the expedition?" I asked gently.

"All the time," Zora replied. "It made life uncomfortable for the rest of us. The two have known each other forever, but rather than being friends, they were professional rivals. They once wrote a book together, but Milo received the lion's share of publicity from it, and their relationship never recovered."

"Was the book about the death worm?"

"No. It was about the chupacabra. It destroyed the credibility of the witnesses claiming to have seen the creature, and it shot down the entire myth. The book sold really well but was not popular among the cryptid community."

"Oh, my," I said. "I've met a chupacabra, and he would not be happy to hear about this book."

She stared at me with her mouth open. "You what?"

"Forget what I said. I'm not supposed to talk about Chuck."

"Do you know of anyone who would kill Claire Fusseldink?" Matt asked Zora to get the ball rolling again.

"Of course not. I'd heard her death was accidental—a poisoning of some sort."

"Did the Fusseldinks have a healthy marriage?"

"I didn't know them well enough to judge, but I'd heard the marriage was under a great strain because of Milo's constant travel and his obsession with his career."

"Let me ask you a hypothetical question," I said. "If Dr. Fusseldink found a Mongolian Death Worm when he was alone, would he have the means to smuggle the worm out of Mongolia without the expedition knowing about it?"

Zora laughed.

"What's so funny?" I asked.

"The logistics of that would be exceedingly difficult. But even if Milo could pull it off all by himself, he would never do so. Not in a million years. He wanted fame. He wanted to be in the spotlight. If he had found the worm, he'd make sure every single person in the world knew about it."

I DROVE us back east along Alligator Alley, the straight-as-an-arrow world of humans, asphalt, and autos. It was hemmed in by fences just past the shoulder that prevented drivers from losing control and plunging into the world of reptiles, insects, wetlands, and brutal food chains. We eventually ended up on I-95 northbound toward Jellyfish Beach, passing through urbanized Southeast Florida, until we escaped the sprawl and enjoyed a view of trees and fields once again.

While my eyes took in the scenery, Matt's were glued to his phone. He was scrolling through messages in his newspaper's collaboration app.

"So, I think someone from the expedition captured the

worm," I said. "They smuggled it back to the US and planted it in the Fusseldink's bedroom to attack Claire. Milo had a motive —a bad marriage and lots of money to inherit. If his dead body is somewhere in the Gobi Desert, he obviously couldn't have done it. I need to find out if he's alive and where he is. And we should dig deeper to see if anyone else on the expedition had a motive to kill Claire."

Matt grunted in agreement, his attention still on his phone.

"What's so exciting at *The Jellyfish Beach Journal* on your day off?" I needled him.

"Oh, not much. Just a suspicious death, that's all."

"Suspicious, how?"

"I think our Mongolian Death Worm has struck again."

CHAPTER 3
DIE WITH A SMILE

At Matt's urging, I didn't take the exit to Jellyfish Beach. Instead, I took the next one and headed west toward Mullet City, home of the Crab County Medical Examiner's Office. In other words, the morgue. Matt filled me in on the little he'd learned so far.

"A body was found on the beach this morning. The death was initially blamed on natural causes. But I made some inquiries about it, in light of the Fusseldink death."

"Why?"

"Because this one happened on the beach."

"So?"

"*Sand*," he said, as if I were a child. "You know, the stuff that covers the ground in the Gobi Desert?"

"That's a big leap."

"Yeah, well, I just found out from the Medical Examiner that the victim's face has the same burns that you described on Claire Fusseldink. You said you feared the death worm had escaped from her house. What if it's living beneath the sand on the beach?"

Where this was going finally dawned on me. "That would be bad news."

"Exactly. Luckily, Dr. Ramirez agreed to meet with me."

"Wow. A local official you haven't alienated. Yet."

"Save the sarcasm for later, okay?"

"I'll try. If you promise to keep quiet about the worm. The Society wouldn't want the police and Animal Control trying to kill the creature. Let's see if the police come up with alternative suspects."

When we arrived at the morgue, the front-desk clerk pointed to the ME's office down a short hall.

"Hi, Dr. Ramirez," Matt said, shaking hands with the stout older woman. "Thanks for seeing us at such short notice. This is my colleague, Missy Mindle."

Ramirez sat at her desk and directed us to take the two chairs facing it. "I'm surprised you're interested in the case."

"As well as the poisoning earlier this week."

She frowned. "I admit they're almost identical. We've completed the autopsy in the Fusseldink case and received the toxicology report. I'm confident this new case will present similar results."

"Who was the latest victim?" I asked.

Ramirez frowned again. "A middle-aged woman with the surname Nguyen."

"Is her age close to Mrs. Fusseldink's?"

"Yes. Based on her attire, she was jogging on the beach in the pre-dawn hours."

"Jogging causes vibrations in the ground," Matt said to me in a low voice.

I ignored him. "Was the victim already deceased when she was found?"

Ramirez nodded. I wondered if the similarity in ages was only a coincidence. Perhaps a serial killer was preying on women who resembled Claire.

"Did she have yellowish acid burns on her face?" Matt asked.

"Yes. From the toxin that we determined was the cause of death. The burn pattern indicated that a liquid had been sprayed on her. It was a neurotoxin, affecting her nervous system."

I asked, "Did she happen to have a smile on her face?"

Ramirez looked at me strangely. "Funny you would ask that. Her facial muscles were indeed frozen in a smile. My theory is that the smile was a response to the toxin itself, which we haven't yet identified. I've never seen anything like it before. The toxin is quite exotic. It has similarities in composition to viper venom but doesn't match that of any known reptile. We also found molecular structures resembling those of the alkaloids found in raw opium. The victim could have experienced pleasure while suffering from the skin burns and the respiratory distress leading to cardiac arrest."

"I've always wanted to die with a smile on my face," Matt said. "But not this way."

I ignored him again. "Doctor, where do you think the toxin came from?" I asked, despite being fairly certain it had come from the death worm. I hoped law enforcement would develop a different theory.

"I don't have a clue," she replied. "All I can say is that it's natural and not manmade."

"Manmade?"

"A notorious local poisoner has been released from prison on parole, and the Jellyfish Beach Police Department is taking a keen interest in his recent activities. I doubt he was responsible for these deaths, but that is not my job, is it?"

"I suppose not."

"Thank you for the information you shared," Matt said, rising from his chair. "I appreciate your transparency."

We left the morgue and headed east to Jellyfish Beach. Matt used the time to call Detective Shortle. Surprisingly, she answered.

"Hi Detective," Matt said, putting his phone on speaker. "I have Missy Mindle on the line with me. We heard that you have a suspect in the two recent poisonings. Is that correct?"

"Rosen, you know I won't comment on ongoing investigations." Coming through the phone's speakers, her voice was even colder than usual.

"But surely you can give me some information off the record?"

"A poisoner has left prison and returned to Jellyfish Beach. Two fatal poisonings have since occurred. We're simply using due diligence to gather facts."

"The medical examiner said the toxin used in both deaths was created naturally. So how can this poisoner be responsible?"

"I didn't say I'm certain he was responsible. And, off the record, you can milk snakes for their venom, or get it from other natural sources, and then use it as you wish."

“Um, yeah, but—”

“I’ve cooperated with you, so I expect you to do the same with me. There’s no reason for you and Missy to behave like amateur sleuths. I’ve got this investigation under control, and I’ll share with you any new developments so you can report them. Understood?”

“Sure. But—”

“Don’t impede my investigation. That’s an order and a warning.”

“She hung up on me,” Matt griped.

“This is good,” I said. “No one is talking about Mongolian Death Worms. We can continue to search for whoever brought the worm here. We won’t get in Shortle’s way because our investigation is different from hers.”

“For the moment. But if we bump into her again, she won’t be happy.”

THE SUN WAS low in the sky when we finally returned to Jellyfish Beach. When I pulled up in front of Matt’s bungalow, I felt romantic tension flare up out of nowhere. Matt and I had been in strict business mode all day, and the thought of a deadly cryptid on the loose in our town was not exactly an aphrodisiac.

But the fact was, Matt and I had recently consecrated our attraction to each other that had been simmering for years. We were best friends and loved each other. For Matt, it was a let’s-get-married kind of love. For me, it was a bit more complicated.

I had, perhaps unwisely, offered a friends-with-benefits arrangement. And finally, it had kicked off spectacularly.

But now what?

Matt remained in the passenger seat. "Um, would you like to come in?" He seemed uncomfortable. "You know, for a drink. And dinner, maybe? I have some frozen leftovers."

"I don't know. After a trip to the morgue, I'm not in peak socializing mode."

"Yeah, I understand. We can do things other than socialize."

"I'm not in the mood for those, either."

He seemed relieved. "Yeah, it's been a long day."

I was relieved that he was relieved. But not exactly happy about it. "I also need to get home and feed the iguana and the cats."

"Yes, of course."

I considered inviting him to follow me home for dinner at my place. But suddenly, a high-pitched buzzing filled my brain.

My security wards had been triggered. My magical version of a burglar alarm was telling me someone had broken into my home. Specifically, someone evil.

"My wards just went off," I said. "I need to get home."

"Let me come with you for safety."

"Thanks for offering, but I know exactly who's in my house. Ruth."

Matt visibly shuddered. He had recently endured abuse-by-magic by my biological mother, a black-magic sorceress who had given me up for adoption when I was a baby. "Yeah, I think I'll pass. I doubt she intends to hurt you tonight."

"Now that she knows I'm her perfect acolyte."

We kissed goodbye. It was more passionate that I'd expected, leaving me tingling and reconsidering asking Matt to follow me. The feeling didn't last. He got out of the car, and I headed home to find out why Mrs. Evil Incarnate was in my house.

THE SUN HAD SET by the time I arrived, and all the lights were blazing from my windows, even though I normally kept only a single lamp on, plugged into a timer. I parked in the driveway and stormed to the front door in a foul mood. The door was unlocked, and as I expected, I was greeted by the reek of cigarette smoke.

"How many times have I told you not to smoke in my house?" I shouted.

"No need to scream," said Ophelia Lawthorne, aka Ruth Bent, sitting on the living room couch with a beer in one hand and a cigarette in the other. "My hearing is still reasonably good."

I shut the door behind me and glared at her. "You obviously used magic to unlock the door. Why didn't you use any to disable my wards?"

"Because I wanted you to know you had a very important visitor waiting for you."

"Why is this VIP breaking into my home tonight?"

"You missed your training session yesterday."

"Something important came up. Look, I attended the

meeting last week. I even brought donuts as required of the newbie in your coven. Can't you cut me some slack?"

"You sound like a teenager."

"You wouldn't know. You weren't around when I was a teen. And I'm thankful for that fact."

Ruth cackled, letting out a phlegmy cough. "I'm here now for you, dearie."

"You're here trespassing."

"Checking to see why you missed your training session. You're on the cusp of becoming a powerful sorceress. You were born with good magical genes, and you've taken white magic as far as it can go. When you embrace black magic, you will move to an entirely different level. Doesn't that excite you?"

It did, to be honest. I was like an athlete who had reached her peak and was considering using performance-enhancing drugs to extend her limits. In most sports, they were illegal, though in some they were in a gray area. With the drugs, I could achieve unbelievable feats. But my honor would be tarnished.

More smoke drifted into the living room, followed by Tony the iguana marching in on his splayed legs, a cigarette clenched in his mouth.

"Tony! What the heck are you doing?" I scolded.

"If this old bat can smoke inside, why can't I?" he asked in his New York accent.

"Smoking will stunt your growth, you little green freak," Ruth muttered.

"I'm your witch's familiar and I'm here to protect you," Tony said to me. "Your feline furballs, who you love more than me, are cowering under your bed right now. You need an animal with cojones."

"How are you going to protect me? Ruth is a black-magic sorceress."

"I'm here to protect your honor." He turned to Ruth. "Stop trying to tempt Missy with your promises of more powerful magic. She doesn't want to sully herself with evil."

The little bugger must have read my mind.

"You're rather cocky for a freaking lizard," Ruth said. "Your trainers magically enhanced your mind and gave you vocal cords, but you don't impress me at all. You might make a decent iguana stew, though."

She pointed both hands at him, and I felt a rush of magical energy shoot from them. Tony staggered backward, then ran from the room like a frightened cat.

"What did you do to him?" I demanded.

"Just a little spell to punish you and him both."

Tony was talking excitedly to someone in the garage.

"What's going on out there?"

"That annoying lizard was mouthing off to me," Ruth replied. "So, I cast a spell that will make him unable to stop mouthing off to everyone. Neither of you will have a moment of peace and quiet."

"You made your point," I said. "I'll show up for the next training session. Please break your spell."

"I'll break it after you show up for your session. Thursday at two o'clock."

My temptation to flirt with greater power was gone now, replaced by anger and resentment. Fred Furman and the werewolf merchants of the town had begged me to infiltrate Ruth's coven to help them battle her and her Mafia-like demands for protection money. As a result, I had to endure Ruth's ridiculous loyalty tests.

Ruth stood up to go. "Will I see you on Thursday?"

"Yeah."

"You meant to say, 'Yes, Your Holiness.'"

"Yes, Your Holiness."

I seethed with anger. There must be a way to get revenge on her. I could suggest to Shortle that Ruth had used black magic to poison the two victims of the death worm. Shortle might buy the tale because she had questioned whether I had killed Claire with magic.

No, I couldn't frame an innocent person. I mean, Ruth was hardly innocent; but I doubted she had anything to do with the poisonings. How could I have even considered being so dishonest?

Tony, who hadn't stopped talking to himself in the garage, returned to the living room. "I've got tons of stuff I need to get off my chest."

"Now is not the best time."

But he began to unload on me all his grievances amassed during his centuries-long existence as a familiar, from the sixteenth century until today, from being in the body of a dog to his current existence as a lizard, and everything in between.

"Why did the magic-familiar breeding facility give you vocal cords?" I asked him. "Why? What's wrong with communicating telepathically?"

"It's easier to keep your attention when I can talk out loud."

He followed me around the house as I fed the cats, made a pasta dinner for myself, and got ready for bed. When I turned off the light in my bedroom, he was sitting on my nightstand, chattering away about some mage a hundred years ago who hadn't shown him enough respect. He didn't stop talking for a single second all night long. I barely slept, and for the few moments I did, my dreams were filled with complaints delivered in a New York accent.

Okay, maybe I would frame Ruth after all. See, black magic stained everyone it touched.

CHAPTER 4

ICKY THINGS

I awoke to loud, angry hissing. Bubba and Brenda were beside me on the bed, pulsating with anger.

And there was muttering in a New York accent. Tony was on my nightstand, talking to himself.

"Oh, you're finally awake," he said. "I had a dream about my childhood. Puppyhood, I should say—when I was a King Charles Cavalier Spaniel in Spain four hundred years ago."

"I don't care," I mumbled. "It's too early. Let me go back to sleep."

"No, this was a traumatic dream, and I can't get over it. It'll be therapeutic to talk it out."

"Talk to the cats in another room."

"They hate me. Which is another grievance I want to discuss. But not now. I gotta talk about my dream. It was a memory of when the wizard turned me into a witch's familiar. There I was, just a little puppy with my littermates, when I was plucked from a world of innocence to a complicated existence of humans and magic. It was a nightmare, I tell ya."

"Poor little puppy." I rolled over with my back to him. "I'm going back to sleep."

"You've got to let me get this stuff off my chest. It was the most traumatic event in my life, for Pete's sake. Not counting the time I was reincarnated as an iguana. Oh, man, that brings back painful memories, too. Being a cold-blooded reptile ain't easy, for sure."

"You've been talking nonstop since Ruth hexed you last night. Give me some space."

"How can you be so uncaring? I'm your familiar. Your partner."

"I don't have a partner," I said, a little too forcefully. Matt hadn't yet reached partner status, and I felt kind of guilty about it.

"Your partner in magic. That's what I am, which brings up a whole other topic we need to discuss."

"Please, just let me sleep a little longer."

The doorbell rang. I fumbled for my phone and looked at the doorbell camera. Yeah, using technology, not magic. No surprise, Mrs. Lupis and Mr. Lopez stood on my front porch, dark figures silhouetted by the tenuous rays of first light behind them. I sighed loudly, dragged myself out of bed, and stepped into a pair of sweatpants, keeping on my wrinkled sleeping T-shirt. I stomped angrily out of the bedroom, sending the cats into hiding under the bed.

I opened the front door, and my two handlers said, "Good morning," in cheery voices, although they weren't smiling.

"We have a problem on our hands," Mrs. Lupis said.

"It requires your immediate attention," said Mr. Lopez.

"Why me?"

"May we come in?" Mrs. Lupis asked. She appeared confused by the lack of my usual hospitality.

"Yes, of course. Sorry. I'm exhausted and not quite awake."

I led them to the kitchen and put a kettle on to boil. They sat at the table while I perched on a stool beside the island counter.

Mr. Lopez opened his attaché case and glanced at some documents. "There has been another killing."

"Yeah, I heard."

He looked at me with surprise.

"Remember, my. . ." I paused, not sure if I should call Matt my boyfriend or partner. "My friend is a reporter. He told me about it. A poisoning at the beach."

"We feel strongly that the Mongolian Death Worm was responsible," Mrs. Lupis said. "Obviously, it escaped from the Fusseldink home after killing Claire. We expected it to hide in the sands of the beach, but not to kill again so soon."

"Vibrations," I said. "Some searchers in Mongolia sent vibrations into the ground to get the worms to rise to the surface. They were unsuccessful, but I think they were correct in their theory. The woman who was killed on the beach had been jogging and probably ran near the worm's hiding place. It can't burrow too deeply before reaching the water table, unlike in the Gobi Desert. The pounding of her footsteps brought the worm to the surface."

"Why did it attack?" Mr. Lopez asked. "The jogger had

probably already passed the worm by the time it came out of the sand."

"Perhaps she turned around and was jogging back to where she had started," Mrs. Lopez suggested.

"Yeah. It was before dawn," I said, "and this large mammal was thundering toward the worm. It squirted her with venom in self-defense."

"You both have convincing explanations," Mr. Lopez said. "But they only illustrate the problem we have here. Namely, lots of humans visit the beach this time of year, and there will be more encounters between the worm and the large mammals we call humans. Consequently, there will be more deaths. We must capture the worm immediately."

"What time do you need to be at work this morning?" Mrs. Lupis asked me.

"It's not my turn to open the store today, but I ought to be there by ten or so."

"Then we mustn't dally. Drive us to the Cryptid Sanctuary. The Society has the world's leading expert on the death worm, and we must collaborate with him."

"How come I'm the one who always has to drive there?" I complained, although I already knew the answer. My handlers weren't human and couldn't get driver's licenses. I hurriedly fed Tony and the cats, threw on some clothes, and got into my car with my passengers.

The Cryptid Sanctuary was where injured and ill cryptids received medical care before being released back into the wild or, depending on what species they were, back into human society. Many creatures lived there permanently because they were too dangerous to humans or had other reasons that made them a poor fit for the real world.

The sanctuary existed in a parallel universe, hidden within a national wildlife preserve, where it was impossible for humans to access. As the human population grew, more cryptids needed to take refuge at the sanctuary. The place continually expanded with the aid of magic and funding from Lord-knows-who. In fact, I had never gotten a straight answer as to how the Society was funded at all. I guessed billionaire cryptids were responsible.

The sun had fully risen as we entered the preserve where the sanctuary was hidden. We passed two cyclists on the narrow asphalt road. The road curved sharply, and I turned off into a bed of ferns next to a cypress tree. There was no sign of the hidden drive I had entered; I only knew it was there because of prior visits. The tingling in my gut told me it was a magical road, impossible for regular humans to use.

We bumped along the drive—more of a trail, really—past longleaf pines and saw palmettos, until we reached a narrow creek. Going against my normal instincts, I drove across the creek and ascended the opposite bank until my car was blocked by a solid wall of sawgrass taller than the car.

The wall magically opened. I drove the car into the opening, along a path that was revealed by the grass continually parting in front of us as we moved forward. The landscape opened into a giant meadow invisible to any airplanes or drones flying overhead. The meadow was bordered by a stone wall topped with a wrought-iron fence. We passed through a monumental gate that swung open automatically next to a sign that announced, "Welcome to the Cryptid Sanctuary, administered by the Friends of Cryptids Society of the Americas."

Several buildings surrounded by elaborately manicured landscaping covered the grounds of what resembled a cross between a luxury resort and a college campus. There was a visitors' center with interactive educational displays, though I couldn't imagine who would visit the place. The other buildings were offices, medical facilities, research labs, classrooms, libraries, recreational amenities, and residences. There were even high-security detention centers for dangerous residents.

I drove past two trolls on a putting green, as Mrs. Lupis directed me to a large office building where I parked out front.

"Dr. Hooey is expecting us."

"That's an unfortunate name for a scientist," I said.

"Not where he comes from."

"Which is where?"

"I'm not at liberty to say."

Dr. Hooey's office and laboratory were on the fourth floor, and he looked very human to me in his lab coat and wide, pleasant face. What didn't look human was his ill-fitting, flax-colored hairpiece.

"It is nice to meet you," he said in a European accent when we were introduced. "Follow me to my office where we can talk."

We passed through a large room filled with aquariums and terrariums. They contained a variety of creatures, including species of worms and snake-like reptiles.

The scientist pointed to a snake coiled on a rock. "Spitting cobra." Then, to a spider on a web. "Southern black widow. Quite venomous."

One tank held what could only be described as a dark-red blob.

"What is that?" I pointed at the blob.

"The Blob," Dr. Hooey replied. "Like from the classic horror movie. We're hoping it won't outgrow the enclosure."

In a nearby terrarium, a snake-like tail twitched from behind a rock.

"Don't look in there," Dr. Hooey warned us. "That's a basilisk. It can kill you just by making eye contact."

"Good to know," I muttered.

"We need to put a warning sign on the tank. Our cleaning crews keep dying."

As we passed a large aquarium with a humming aerator, something thudded against the glass, and I jumped. A giant white worm repeatedly struck the wall and bared giant fangs, one on the upper jaw and one on the lower.

Dr. Hooey glanced back at the tank and smiled fondly. "The legendary Indus from India, first written about by the ancient Greeks. We are so honored to have acquired a specimen. I'm as fond of this creature as I am of the Mongolian Death Worm."

I had no desire to examine any of the other enclosures, so I followed Dr. Hooey through the large room and into his office, with Mrs. Lupis and Mr. Lopez right behind me. Dr. Hooey sat behind a large desk covered with papers, and we took seats facing him.

"Speaking of the Mongolian Death Worm," I said, "I'm told you are the leading expert on it."

He gave a perfunctory smile. "That is kind of you to say. I have studied the worm for decades. I am an ickologist."

"Sorry? You said an ecologist?"

"No, *ick*ologist. I'm an expert in creatures that cause the ick factor—all cryptids and legendary creatures that are icky, creepy, crawly, slimy, nasty, gross, disgusting. The ones in the vivaria out there are among the more dangerous examples. You didn't see our flesh-eating slime bugs. They're quite impressive."

"Sounds like you've found your true calling." I caught myself before saying anything more sarcastic.

"I have indeed. Just because they're icky doesn't mean these creatures don't deserve study and respect."

"I'm not so sure about respect."

"The Mongolian Death Worm inhabits one of the world's most inhospitable environments. It's capable of surviving for weeks without sustenance. It can kill you with its venom, without biting or stinging you, at a distance of up to four meters. The venom has a narcotic effect, so prey that doesn't receive a lethal dose will approach the worm wanting more venom. The worm can also electrocute you with its tail. Those abilities, in anyone's opinion, make the creature worthy of respect."

Mr. Lopez cleared his throat. "As we alerted you, Dr. Hooey, it appears a worm has been brought to America. All evidence points to it having killed a woman in her home before it escaped to the beach. It was living in the sand when it killed a second woman, a jogger."

I mentioned my theory that the vibrations from the jogger's footsteps impelled the worm to burrow to the surface.

"I believe your theory is correct," the ickologist said. He turned his focus to Mrs. Lupis. "Your email said Dr. Milo Fusseldink is involved in this?"

"Yes. His wife was the first victim. Dr. Fusseldink was the co-leader of an expedition that went to Mongolia to search for the worm. He went missing, and his whereabouts are unknown."

"Ah. Interesting. Do you believe Dr. Fusseldink is responsible for this worm?"

"Yes," I said. The conviction in my voice made everyone stare at me curiously. "I believe he smuggled the worm home, and he placed it like a booby trap to attack his wife. Their marriage was not in good shape, from what I've heard."

"Do you have any evidence that he is guilty?"

"Nope. Nada."

Dr. Hooey frowned at me. "It goes against my ethics to speak ill of a colleague when there's no evidence of wrongdoing."

"I've been wondering. Why didn't the Friends of Cryptids Society pay for the Mongolian expedition?" I asked. After all, the Society appeared to have bottomless cash. "Isn't Dr. Fusseldink a member?"

"He's a member," Mrs. Lupis replied. "He pays a membership fee every year and receives our newsletter."

"And a free tote bag," Mr. Lopez added cheerfully.

"But he's not an employee," Mrs. Lupis continued. "Cryptozoologists like him do their own thing. They're addicted to self-promotion and the acolytes it attracts. They share the Society's mission, but they have their own agendas."

"And they're human," said Mr. Lopez. "The Society doesn't hire humans as full-time employees. Only as associates, like you."

I already knew that my handlers weren't human. I looked at Dr. Hooey. He nodded slightly.

So, what were these "people" I was speaking with who weren't humans? They obviously could shift to human form, but from which species? Or were they of multiple species?

Mr. Lopez looked at me with a smile. "I see the cogs of your brain spinning. All will be revealed to you when the time is appropriate."

"Okay. Dr. Hooey, how do you suggest we catch the escaped worm? Or worms?"

"You've learned how impossible it is to catch them in the Gobi Desert, their natural habitat. In Jellyfish Beach, you have two advantages. For one, all the human feet pounding the sand and creating vibrations."

"Before they become victims," Mr. Lopez said under his breath.

"Right. Make that three advantages. The second being all the humans creating an ample food supply. The third is fresh water. It is said that the worms come out at night during the incredibly rare rainstorms in the Gobi Desert. At the beaches here, there is no fresh water, but there are more frequent rainstorms, even now during the dry season. You must constantly patrol the beaches during such storms to see if the worm comes to the surface."

"How far from the Fusseldink's home could the worm have traveled?" I asked.

"Most likely less than a mile," Dr. Hooey replied. "And you can try other tactics, such as leaving open containers of fresh water on the beach at night. Perhaps they will attract it."

"Thank you for the advice."

"And one more piece of advice. You should hurry with your search," the ickologist said. "Because the death worm has one other ability you should know about: parthenogenesis."

Mrs. Lupis and Mr. Lopez gasped in horror.

"What does that mean?" I asked.

"Reproduction without a mate. You might soon have more than one death worm to worry about."

CHAPTER 5
BACHELOR PAD

After leaving the sanctuary, I dropped my handlers off at a nail salon (don't ask) and managed to get to the botanica by 10:00 a.m. A miracle. But I was a wreck from the lack of sleep thanks to Tony and my early visitors.

When I returned home after work, I fed all the animals, gulped down a frozen microwaved meal, and hit the sack early, hoping to catch up on my sleep. How could I have been so naïve?

"You're welcome to talk about your grievances, too," Tony said from my bedside table in the darkness. "Just let me reckon with a few more of my issues first."

"Please, Tony, no. Not tonight. I need to sleep."

"Of course. But do you know what it's like to sleep in someone's garage—no heat, no AC—while the stupid cats are comfy as bugs in a rug in your bedroom every night?"

I didn't reply. I tried to ignore him. But the loquacious lizard wouldn't shut up for one moment all night long. Perhaps

I had brief moments of unconsciousness amid the constant complaining. However, actual snoozing was not in the cards that night.

My lack of sleep made me a zombie the following day, working at the botanica. That's not hyperbole. An actual zombie, Carl, stopped by and when he saw the dark circles around my eyes, he moaned in sympathy. I watched him shuffle down the aisles behind Madame Tibodet as she gathered supplies for her voodoo ceremonies. I envied the simple, undead existence of Carl compared to my crazy, complicated life.

Somehow, I made it through the day with a minimum of mistakes, although in my stupor I nearly stepped on Daisy, our resident blue land crab—sorry, *were*-land crab—who gave me a warning pinch on my ankle before scuttling out of my way. I wished I felt fresher, because that night I had magic to perform.

"What if the neighbors see us break in?" Matt asked as we sat in his truck, parked in front of the dark Fusseldink house. "There's still crime-scene tape across the door."

"That's why I asked you to bring cleaning supplies. When they see us walking in with a mop and vacuum, they'll assume we're cleaners. They won't pay us any mind."

"What if the police pass by? Can you use your invisibility spell?"

"I need to conserve my magical energy for my locator spell. Stop worrying and let's go inside."

We grabbed the cleaning tools from the truck bed and climbed the tall stairs to the front door. The ocean winds had battered the crime-scene tape so badly that it no longer blocked the door, so I went straight to work on my unlocking spell. The lock was state-of-the-art, but I defeated it after a few minutes.

We didn't want to push our luck with the neighbors by turning on lights. However, enough moonlight streamed through the windows to allow us to navigate through the common areas to the main bedroom. Milo's dresser drawer was still partly open, and I took out the old-fashioned wooden hair-brush. It held several gray hairs and was brimming with psychic energy.

"Please wait in the living room," I said to Matt. "Keep an eye out for any unwanted visitors."

Forcing myself to ignore the dazzling view of the moon reflecting off the ocean outside, I knelt on the floor and pulled supplies from my tote bag. I used a dry-erase marker to draw a magic circle around me and placed candles on the five points of an imagined pentagram inside the circle where they touched its circumference.

"Hey, Missy!" Matt called from the living room. "I heard something."

I sighed in frustration at the interruption. "What?"

"A scratching noise. Do you think the worm is still in the house?"

I got up off the floor and went to the living room. Matt was standing on the coffee table by the sofa.

"Did you forget the worm killed someone on the beach? Why would it be here?"

The word *parthenogenesis* in the ickologist's voice echoed in my head. Had the worm created offspring before it escaped the house?

"Listen!" Matt whispered excitedly. "Do you hear that?"

A scratching sound came from behind the loveseat. It sounded like the noise I had heard when the worm was loose in the house after killing Claire. But not exactly the same. I cautiously approached the loveseat and peered behind it.

Matt had dumped our decoy cleaning gear here: a mop, broom, vacuum, and a couple of tote bags—none of which would be used for any housecleaning. One of the tote bags held extra candles and other spell-casting gear of mine.

The bag moved.

"There's something in my tote bag!" I whispered. It was more of a croak than a whisper.

Matt rushed to my side. We stared at the bag, frozen with uncertainty, until fear made me step backward, pulling Matt with me. Death worms can spit their venom four meters?

A head shot up from the interior of the bag. Matt squealed.

It was an iguana's head. "You don't mind that I came along, do you?" Tony asked.

"What the heck?" Matt was angry, probably embarrassed by his squealing.

"I had some things I needed to discuss," Tony said. "They couldn't wait for Missy to return home."

"Yes, they can wait," I said in a tone that brooked no arguing. "I have a spell to cast right now and I need *silence*!"

Tony's mouth opened, but no sound came out. I turned and walked back to the bedroom.

Kneeling again inside the magic circle, I held the hairbrush in both hands and regained my concentration. I recited the incantation for the spell as I gathered my internal energies and enhanced them with energy I drew from the five elements represented by the pentagram. The hairbrush grew warm, almost hot. As I chanted the words of the spell, I focused on the psychic energy Milo had left on the brush. I pulled the energy inward and combined it with the growing power inside me.

The incantation was complete, and magic flowed from me, coalescing into a glowing orb that floated at eye level a couple of feet from my head. It was a manifestation of Milo's psychic energy, connected to my own. Like a law of physics, it sought to reunite itself with Milo's psychic energy inside him. If he were still alive, that is. I pumped more energy into the orb, preparing it for the long journey to Mongolia.

My senses were now connected to the orb, allowing me to see from its perspective. I was staring at my face now, eyes closed, brow furrowed with concentration.

"Go find the soul to which you belong," I told the orb.

It sped away from me and passed through the French doors, over the balcony, and across the beach. I watched the progress as if I were looking at a video from a camera on a drone. The orb reached the ocean and sped past the breakers. *How long*, I wondered, *would it take the orb to make the journey to Mongolia?*

I never got my answer. The orb made a sharp right turn and headed south over the water, parallel to the shore. It whizzed past high-rise condominium buildings, including Squid Tower, where my former vampire patients resided. The high-rises gave way to single-family homes before the ocean inlet appeared. The orb crossed it, then took another sharp right and headed inland.

The small fishing village of Port Inferno was just below. The orb rose slightly in altitude and circled an old, two-story apartment building on the bank of the Intracoastal Waterway. It hovered in front of a ground-floor apartment, 105, passed through the front door, and entered a small, shabby living room.

A bespectacled, bald man with a potbelly sat in a recliner, reading a book. The orb plunged into his chest, like a dog jumping into its owner's lap. My vision went black as I lost my connection with the orb. It had returned to the soul to which it belonged.

The soul of the man I recognized from an old photograph. Milo Fusseldink.

"He's right here in Crab County?" Matt asked after I had broken the spell and joined him in the living room. "Are you sure?"

"Yeah. He's in some dumpy apartment building in Port Inferno. I don't know how long he's been there, but I'm guessing he returned to the US before his wife died."

"You're saying he brought home the worm and put it in their bedroom?"

"I had a hunch it was him," I said. "Didn't you?"

"Sort of. Especially after we learned that he'd inherit a lot of money from his wife. And Zora mentioned their marriage was under strain. But why would he put the worm in his own dresser drawer?"

"We've discussed this already. The worm could obviously wriggle in and out of anywhere it wanted to go in the bedroom. Milo probably had put it in Claire's dresser, or in the bed."

Matt shuddered at the thought. "How do we prove he did it?"

"We need to investigate him. Follow him around if necessary. When we learn enough to back up our theory, we can confront him, and I'll use my truth spell."

"Okay, but we have a dilemma. If he's guilty, how do we make sure he faces justice for murdering his wife? And, I guess, gets charged with involuntary manslaughter for killing the jogger on the beach? We would need to reveal the existence of the worm to explain the deaths."

I sighed. "That's a problem. The Society wants the worm to remain secret, at least until they've captured it for examination and cataloguing."

"There's no way to connect Milo with the murders without the murder weapon—the worm."

"I wonder if he harvested any venom," I said, "like Shortle believes the convicted poisoner did."

"And squirted it on his wife with a spray bottle? Doubtful."

"You're right. Why not just let the worm do all the work?"

"That was surely the plan."

"Can we find out when Milo returned to the US?"

"Not easily," Matt replied. "I'd have to file a Freedom of Information Act request to discover when he passed through customs. The airlines won't give me that info. I think we should ask around at his apartment building and see if his landlord or a neighbor will tell us how long ago he moved in."

"Okay, let's get out of this house before we're caught. We'll visit the apartment tomorrow morning before we go to work and see what we find."

On the ride home, the little window at the rear of the pickup truck's cab slid open.

"Now, back to the topics I need to discuss," Tony said.

The apartment building in Port Inferno had probably been built in the 1960s. It appeared well-maintained, but I doubted the apartments had received any significant updates. There were people who didn't care if their home had worn-out carpeting instead of the latest vinyl flooring. They had more important concerns, such as paying the rent or, in Milo's case, being obsessed with his pseudoscience.

"Not a terrible place," Matt said as we sat in his truck in the building's parking lot. "I don't see a swimming pool, but it has a fishing dock. That's a great amenity."

"In your eyes."

"Yes. And in the eyes of the gentleman fishing from it, whom we will now have a little chat with. We should speak to everyone we can before making contact with Milo himself. If he believes we're onto him, he might go into hiding."

We got out of the truck and walked from the parking lot through an archway that joined two parallel sections of the building. A grassy courtyard separated the sections, and ahead of us, the rising sun shimmered on the surface of the wide Intracoastal Waterway. We crossed a narrow lawn and stepped onto the short dock attached to the seawall. An older black man sat in a folding chair beside two fishing rods resting in short sections of PVC pipe bolted to dock pilings.

"Good morning, sir," Matt said. "How are they biting this morning?"

"They're not. Waiting for the tide to change." His voice was deep and faintly annoyed.

"I was hoping you could help us. We're attorneys looking for a man we believe lives here. His name is Milo Fusseldink. We need to inform him about an inheritance coming his way."

"Don't know anyone by that name."

"He lives in one-oh-five," I said.

The man shook his head. "I seen the man who lives there. Don't know him, though. Chubby little white guy."

"Did he move in recently?" Matt asked. "Or has he lived here for a while?"

The man scratched the stubble on his chin. "I've lived here for two years, and he was already here when I moved in. I don't see him much. He must go out of town a lot."

"Does he get any visitors?"

"You think because I'm retired, I'm some busybody watching all my neighbors?" His tone was mock-offended. "I seen a young woman come by a couple of times. Could be his daughter."

"Is there a manager living here on-site?"

"Yeah. In one-oh-one."

The fishing rod to the man's right twitched, then bent in an inverted U. He yanked it from the rod holder and began reeling. "'Bout damn time."

We thanked him and strolled back to the courtyard.

"I thought Milo had rented this place to go into hiding," I said. "I'm surprised he's been here for so long."

"It's got to be because of marital problems."

Apartment 101 had a small sign beneath the brass numerals that said, "Manager." I knocked on the door. A scowling Hispanic woman opened the door and looked us up and down. "No vacancies here."

"We're inquiring about one of your residents," Matt said. "Milo Fusseldink. We tried reaching him, but he's not home." It was a necessary lie.

"He leaves early every day to go to his office. What do you want with him?"

I perked up. "He has an office? Where is it?"

"I don't know. I think it's in Jellyfish Beach. Did he do something wrong?"

"Not at all," Matt replied. "He has money coming his way, and we needed to verify some information. Do you know when he moved in here?"

She sighed. "Do you really want me to look for the paperwork?"

"Just a rough idea of how long he's been here."

"Five, six years. Five seems right."

"Does he get many visitors?" I asked.

"No, he's out of town a lot. I've seen a young woman come by."

"What did she look like?"

"Blonde. She's just a little thing." She looked at her watch. "Do you need anything else? I got work to do."

"No. Thank you very much," Matt said.

"I'll tell him you came by."

"Please don't. We need to speak with him first and verify some information. We don't want him to be unnecessarily worried."

The manager frowned at us suspiciously before closing the door.

"I want to find his office," I said to Matt. "We're more likely to find evidence relating to the worm there than in his home."

"We'll see about that. After we break into his apartment."

"Surely not in broad daylight?"

"Let's just get it over with. Use your unlocking spell, and we'll make this quick."

"Let's see if there's a back door. All the apartments in both sections face the courtyard, and someone will see us if we go through the front."

We headed toward the street and went around to the rear of the wing where Milo and the manager lived. There was an alley with a dumpster and weeds growing through cracks in the asphalt. Each apartment had a back door with frosted louvered windows beside small windows that were probably for the kitchens and bathrooms.

I cleared my mind and focused on the door locks: one in the handle and a deadbolt above it. My unlocking spell was a bit of a struggle, but at last, I got the door open. The first thing that hit me was a musty smell, as if the air conditioning didn't work well. It was uncomfortably warm as I moved through the narrow galley kitchen, Matt right behind me.

The walls of the living room were covered with shelves laden with dusty books and memorabilia. Same with the darkened bedroom. The objects on the shelves were framed photos of blurry objects I supposed were cryptids spotted in the wild. There were plaster casts of strange footprints, and several unnatural-looking skulls, bones, and teeth on display.

"The Friends of Cryptids Society would have a field day in here," I said.

"Yeah. Don't touch anything."

"Of course not."

Unlike the Fusseldink home on the beach, which was

clean and tastefully decorated, the apartment was a chaos of claustrophobic clutter. More evidence that he and his wife were not compatible. In the center of the room was the horrible brown recliner I had seen with my locator spell. Stacks of books surrounded the chair, along with empty water bottles. This was obviously where Milo spent most of his time.

Matt and I searched for boxes, cases, or luggage that could have carried a worm. We figured it would have been packed in sand that would have signs of worm poop and pee. No such luck. I found a small wooden crate, but it was empty and clean inside. A suitcase in the bedroom closet was the same.

When I left the bedroom, I found Matt staring at a professional-grade camera sitting on a small table beside the brown recliner.

"I know I shouldn't touch it, but it's so tempting," he said.

I handed him a tissue from my purse. "Handle it with this to avoid leaving fingerprints."

Without moving the camera, Matt turned it on, the tissue covering his fingers. He pressed a button, and the screen on the camera's back lit up. We crouched beside the table to see the screen, which showed the most recent photo: a view of the outside of a tent in a desert campground at night. Matt clicked through more photos, and all were of the same tent at different times of night and early morning.

"Don't tell me he expected a worm to wriggle out of the tent," I said.

But as Matt clicked through more photos, we saw what Milo was looking for. A man I recognized as Professor Levings entering and leaving the tent.

And then, a shot of a blonde woman leaving the tent at dawn.

"Zora," I said. "Was Professor Levings having a relationship with his assistant?"

Before Matt could answer, the apartment's front door rattled as a key was inserted into the lock.

CHAPTER 6

MONSTERS IN STORAGE

Matt and I looked at each other in terror. Milo was about to enter his apartment and catch us.

We jumped up, raced to the kitchen, and fled through the back door. On the way out, I locked the doorknob manually, but I would need to cast a spell to lock the deadbolt from the outside.

The sound of the front door slamming shut told us there was no time for magic, no time for anything other than leaving the alley and making it to the parking lot without being seen.

"He's going to notice the deadbolt is unlocked," I said, once we were safe in Matt's truck and driving away.

"And I forgot to turn the camera off. Milo will know that someone was looking at his creepy surveillance photos."

"I hope his neighbor and landlord don't tell him we were asking about him." A thought came to me as we headed north toward home. "But maybe that's a good thing if they do."

Matt glanced at me. "Are you crazy?"

"We need to search his office, too, but have no way of finding where it is. If he has something incriminating there, he'll want to check on it, now that he knows someone broke into his apartment."

"Unless he thinks petty thieves broke in."

"Thieves wouldn't check what's on his camera and then leave it behind. Turn around. We're going back to his apartment now. And hurry."

"Why?"

"We're going to follow him if he leaves. He might lead us to his office."

As soon as Matt parked on the street across from the apartment building, Milo passed beneath the archway to the courtyard and entered the parking lot. I gave Matt a smirk of vindication. He shrugged. Milo got into an SUV and drove past Matt's truck without noticing us. The SUV sped in the direction of Jellyfish Beach. We followed at a safe distance.

"What if he's not going to his office?" Matt asked. "He could be going for coffee."

"Just keep following him."

I expected Milo to head to a section of Jellyfish Beach, west of downtown, where most of the commercial office space was located. Instead, he turned onto a side street south of the city and into the entrance of a self-storage complex with a sign advertising climate-controlled units.

We parked on the side street and walked into the complex's driveway. I quickly realized it was the type of storage facility where you must go inside to access your unit. How could we observe which one was Milo's without him noticing us?

"I need to cast my invisibility spell," I whispered to Matt.

"Just on myself. It would take twice as much energy to cover both of us."

"I'll take the hint and wait in the truck."

I stepped behind a wall, out of the view of the facility's front door, and worked quickly to cast the spell. It was one I had devised with the help of Tony and Don Mateo's ghost. The spell blocked the light waves that bounce off objects and enable eyes to see the objects. It required its incantation to be recited perfectly. So afterwards, I checked my entire body with my compact mirror, ensuring that all of me was invisible.

Angling the mirror in various directions, I saw no sign of myself in it. How refreshing it was to look at myself in the mirror without being hypercritical.

The main entrance to the facility was a glass door that required a key card to open it, hopefully only during non-business hours. I tried it, and it was unlocked. When I stepped inside, an employee at the rental desk looked up, surprised that the door had opened on its own. He had thick eyeglasses below slicked-back gray hair and was watching a video on a tablet. I tiptoed past the desk as quietly as I could.

The only way to find Milo's unit was to wander through the labyrinth of hallways, past generic metal doors with numbers on them, hoping that Milo had left his door open or that I would see him leaving and locking up. I began to despair until notes from a strange, primitive flute-like instrument drifted down the hall from around a corner ahead of me.

I followed the music, turned the corner, and saw an open door halfway down the hallway. When I reached Unit 35, I gasped in surprise.

Milo sat cross-legged on the floor, playing a wooden,

bulbous instrument in front of a round basket with its top removed. I could only assume a cobra or a reptile of some sort was in the basket. But that wasn't all that surprised me. The storage unit didn't resemble an office at all. It was more like a natural history museum of cryptozoology.

Take the specimens in Milo's apartment and multiply them tenfold. Not only were there shelves filled with bones, teeth, and plaster casts of footprints, but there were also full-size taxidermy creatures. A furry skunk ape, about seven feet tall, stood glaring at me with glass eyes. Florida's version of Sasquatch looked authentic, but it had to be artificial, right?

A similarly realistic looking chupacabra stood in the corner, snarling menacingly. This had to be a fake because Milo and Professor Levings had cowritten a book debunking the eyewitness claims about the creature. Well, just because the witnesses were wrong didn't mean chupacabras weren't real. I knew they were.

Beside it stood a monster on two hoofed feet. It had wings like a dragon's, a forked tail, and the head of a goat. It resembled a photograph I'd seen in the Society's catalogue of creatures. This was the legendary Jersey Devil, believed to live in the Pine Barrens of New Jersey. With so many humans moving to Florida from the state, I was not surprised to see a Jersey cryptid here.

The walls of the storage unit, where they were not covered by steel shelves, displayed large, framed photos of alleged creature sightings, such as the Loch Ness Monster, Bigfoot, and elf-like beings among trees.

Milo's "office" took my breath away. But it was also unsettling to see the nuttiness of this man's world and realize that it mirrored my own. Yes, working for the Friends of Cryptids Society made me a kook like Milo, though my world had more supernatural creatures in it than his.

But inside this room, I didn't see a hint of the Mongolian Death Worm.

"Hey, what's going on here?" asked the man from the front desk, who had suddenly appeared behind me. "There'd better not be a cobra in that basket. It's against the rules."

He must have followed me here, but how? Then I remembered that though I was invisible, I could still create a shadow. The man must have seen my shadow move past the front door. The fluorescent lights on the hallway ceilings wouldn't have cast distinctive shadows, but the man had probably just wandered around the facility in search of an explanation for the front door opening on its own and the shadow of me the sun had created there.

"Yes, I am employing the method used by snake charmers in India. But this is not a cobra," Milo said. "It's not even a snake. This is a glass lizard."

The employee stepped into the storage unit, nearly bumping into me. "Looks like a snake to me. And it doesn't seem to appreciate your music."

"It's actually a species of lizard without legs. Very common in North America."

"Whatever it is, you're not supposed to have it in here. No pets. No lizards without legs."

"I'm conducting an important experiment," Milo explained. "I have a hypothesis that musical notes at a certain key and pitch, vibrating at a certain frequency, can rouse reptiles like this, which is not dissimilar to the Mongolian

Death Worm. Many cryptozoologists believe the death worm is a reptile, not one of the invertebrate species called worms."

"No, no, no. You can't have death worms here, either."

"Don't be absurd, man! Mongolian Death Worms can only be found in Mongolia. I'm trying to develop a more efficient way of capturing them."

A more efficient way, I thought. *Does that mean he wants to capture another one?*

"Why would you want to catch anything called a death worm?" the employee asked. "Or a death-anything?"

"Because the *allghoi khorkhoi* is a remarkable species. And a delightfully deadly one."

The man cleared his throat loudly. "You know, I have the authority to cancel your lease here. Our tenants store furniture and boxes of papers in our carefully controlled climate of seventy-five degrees and only twenty percent humidity. They don't store weird stuff like gorilla mannequins."

"That's a skunk ape."

"If you want to keep it here, you've got to remove the legless lizard."

Out of nowhere, my stomach growled. Loudly.

Both men looked in my direction.

"That wasn't me," Milo said. "I had breakfast this morning."

"Me too," said the employee. "And I take those weight-loss shots that make me hardly ever hungry."

That's what I get for skipping breakfast in favor of breaking into a man's apartment, I thought. Moving slowly, I eased down the hall away from the two men.

My stomach gurgled again, dramatically, musically, like a song of sadness.

The employee stepped out of the storage unit, unsuccessfully trying to see the source of the plaintive wail. It was long past the time to leave the facility. I was going to be late for work. Especially because I was going to stop for a bagel on the way.

A SECOND VISIT to the storage facility was necessary now that I had Milo's unit number. It had to be done when Milo wasn't there, of course, but I didn't want to do it in the middle of the night.

"It would be too much trouble at night," I told Matt over the phone. "I'd need a spell to unlock the main entrance, but that might trigger an alarm because a key card wasn't used. Plus, I'd have to cast a spell to pause the security cameras, and that might trigger something. There might even be a security guard on site."

"So, what are you going to do?"

"Use your big mouth to my advantage."

"Huh?"

"We'll show up during business hours. I'll be invisible and follow you through the main entrance doors. Then, you'll distract the employee, keeping him at the front desk while I break into Milo's storage unit and search it."

"*Big mouth*?"

"Outgoing personality with aggressive journalistic instincts."

"That sounds a *little* better. But. . ."

"Okay. How about: your natural dazzling charm can distract anyone? Pick me up at the botanica this afternoon at four."

The annoying guy with the thick glasses and slicked-back hair was at the front desk when Matt entered the storage building. I should say, when *we* entered. I was invisible again and followed him as closely as I could to avoid casting strange shadows. Matt approached the desk and inquired about renting a unit. I slipped quietly down the hall.

Milo's unit was secured with a padlock, which could be a challenge for my particular unlocking spell. I eventually got inside, closed the door behind me, and turned on the overhead fluorescent tubes.

I had to hand it to Milo. He took a generic concrete room with nothing but an HVAC vent near the ceiling and turned it into . . . an altar of freakiness. His apartment had been constrained by the necessity of having a comfy chair, a kitchen, and a bed. The storage unit was filled with nothing but pure personal obsessions.

I'd already mentioned the taxidermy creatures (or were they simply mannequins?), the photos of cryptids (were they authentic?), the plaster casts of footprints, the bones and teeth, etcetera. I hadn't even mentioned the piles of old VHS tapes and boxes of DVDs. The stacks of photo albums. And the shelves groaning with hardcover journals.

Best of all were the stacks of cardboard specimen boxes that I hastily opened. They contained specimens you wouldn't want to display on shelves because they were too fragile or too disgusting. I won't describe the latter items other than to say they were mummified body parts from non-human creatures. Plus, pelts with unrecognizable kinds of fur. And bones that looked too human-like to leave where anyone could see them.

Finally, I worked my way through the stacks to a newish-looking box and opened it. Inside was a delicate length of shed snakeskin. The snake's body had been thicker than most and about the length of my arm.

My eyes drifted to a label glued to the inside of the box's lid with a caption handwritten in black ink:

Molted skin of an adult Mongolian Death Worm.

CHAPTER 7

THE TEMPTATION OF MISSY

I was tempted to take the boxed death-worm skin with me as evidence, but I didn't want to alert Milo that he was under surveillance. We'd already been too sloppy with the camera and the deadbolt at his apartment. Also, the guy at the front desk would see the box seemingly float through the air and out the door of the facility. I didn't have time to cast an invisibility spell on it.

When I reached the front desk, Matt was clearly stalling, pretending to study a price list for storage units. I came up behind him, rubbed his back to alert him I was there, and followed him outside.

"Any luck?" he asked as we drove away.

I told him about the skin. "Remember, Zora mentioned that the expedition had found a molted skin."

"And it went missing when Milo disappeared."

"Yep. Now we know where the skin is."

"Any chance he brought a live worm from Mongolia in the box which molted while in transit? Did the box have air holes?"

I shook my head before realizing my invisibility hadn't fully dissipated and Matt couldn't see my gesture. "No. It looked like a box for storage, not for transport. But who knows? If the worms can survive buried in the sand, they can probably endure a long journey without fresh oxygen."

"Hmm," Matt stroked his beard. "What you saw was probably just the skin they found lying in the desert. It doesn't mean Milo found a worm."

"True. But it doesn't mean he *didn't* find one."

"Right."

"Look," I said, "this is the best evidence we have so far tying Milo to Claire's death. It's maybe the best we're going to get short of a confession. I'm going to savor this minor victory while I can, okay?"

"You don't need to be testy."

"I'm exhausted. I haven't slept in nights thanks to the talking hex that Ruth put on Tony. And after all the magic I've cast today, I'm drained of energy. Wiped out."

"Sorry. You can sleep at my place if you want."

"Something tells me I won't get much sleep there, either. Anyway, I have a training session with Ruth early tomorrow morning."

"You should blow it off."

"If I did, she would probably kill me."

"Oh."

"Yeah. Welcome to my world."

After yet another night of little to no sleep thanks to my lizard familiar over-sharing every detail of his personal life, I drove to Ruth's apartment filled with dread. It was the opposite of how I'd felt when receiving training from Angela. Unlike Ruth, the powerful mage practiced white magic, like I and most other witches did. She had taught me valuable spells and ways to increase my inherent magical powers, making me a better witch. There was still much more to learn.

Yet I sensed I was nearing the ceiling of my abilities. I doubted that I would ever become as powerful as Angela. I wanted to believe that the session today with Ruth was just to appease her by accepting her demands. The truth was, I was intrigued by my mother's offer to show me the path to power beyond my natural limitations.

This temptation could end badly, I knew. But I had to do this. Or so I told myself.

After I knocked on my mother's apartment door, her manservant Federico let me in. The overweight, middle-aged witch wore his usual red leotard. I'd never learned why he wore that hideous outfit, but it probably involved ritual humiliation.

"Good morning, Missy," he said. "Saint Ruthless is expecting you."

Despite his polite manner, there was anger in his eyes. The last time he'd seen me, Matt punched him out to enable our escape from the apartment.

The place was rarely empty, with coven members usually around. Cult members, to be more accurate. Or there would be local businesspeople she was extorting. But not today. The place looked like a normal apartment, if by normal you meant a horned goat's head painted on the wall above the TV, a sacrificial altar in the dining nook, and numerous black candles everywhere.

Footsteps clicked along the hall leading from the bedrooms, and my mother appeared. The black-magic sorceress wore a floor-length scarlet robe and a matching turban. A large silver pentagram necklace was her only jewelry. The solemnity of her costume was ruined by the cigarette dangling from her mouth.

"Right on time, dearie," she said in her scratchy voice.

"I want to make it clear that I'm not doing anything here today until you break the hex on Tony."

Ruth cackled with amusement. "I can only do that if he's here in front of me."

"I'll go get him. He's in the car."

She seemed disappointed that I'd brought him with me. I went downstairs to my car parked on the street and returned to the apartment with Tony in a pet carrier. He complained from the moment I opened the car door.

"I don't care if you leave your windows partly down," he said. "It's cruel and dangerous to leave a pet in your car in the hell-like heat of our state."

"Florida in January is quite comfortable," I said.

"It doesn't matter. It gets hotter inside cars than the outside temperature. I could have died in there. I should report you to the authorities."

By the time I had returned to the apartment, he was still protesting. "It's legal for someone to break your window to rescue pets left in cars, you know. I wish a good Samaritan had come along and ended my suffering."

"It's time to end *my* suffering. Ruth, honor your promise and break the hex."

"My name is Saint Ruthless."

"My apologies, Saint Ruthless."

"I'm the one who deserves the apologies," Tony said. "Look at me, stuck in this crate like a freakin' furball pet. Can you believe the cruelty and disrespect your daughter had inflicted on me? It's a travesty, I tell ya."

"He really *is* annoying," Ruth said. "Let me shut his trap and then we can begin our session."

"Don't use a silence spell," I begged. "Please, just break the talking hex."

"If I were you, I'd never want to hear this lizard's voice ever again, but I'll do as you ask."

It only took a quick incantation and some hand gestures from her before I felt an icy blast of magic flowing to the pet carrier. Tony was silent.

"How are you feeling, big guy?" I asked.

"Better. Less aggrieved. But don't put me back in your car."

"I'll put you in the kitchen."

"You'd better not," Ruth said. "Federico might turn him into a stew. I'll put him in my spare bedroom, and then we'll begin."

"Don't choose the path of evil," Tony said to me before he was taken away.

For some reason, the darn lizard's words stuck with me.

When Ruth came back to the living room, she ordered me to push furniture against the wall and roll up a musty carpet, revealing an upside-down pentagram painted on the wood flooring. She lit the black candles and turned off the lights.

"You stay in here," she said to Federico, closing the door to the kitchen.

She walked to the end of the room and sat in an ornate chair with her back to the goat's head painting. "Kneel before me."

I shrugged and did as she asked. This training session was merely to satisfy my curiosity. And to keep Ruth from getting angry and killing me. My plan was to feign enough interest in her black magic to mollify her, but not to follow the path past the point of no return.

Besides, the session this morning was nothing like the previous black-magic session I had experienced here. That was when Ruth had originally conjured the demon, Asmodeus, and bound him to me so I could create a doppelgänger of Matt and break him out of jail. That ritual had involved a circle of her acolytes and mysterious powders that she burned.

I gasped as my left palm flared with a burning pain. Blood was oozing from an old, healed wound, as if from a stigmata. I shuddered at the memory of the creation of the wound in the previous ceremony—Ruth slicing my palm with a dagger to draw my blood for the demon.

She cackled from her chair. "Yep, Asmodeus is still bonded to you. In this one demon alone, you'll find more power than you hippie white-magic witches could ever conjure. But you and he are going to have to become closer friends if you want any of that power."

"Um, no thanks. I don't need any new friends."

"I was speaking metaphorically. A demon can't be a friend.

Working with one is like riding a tiger. I'm going to teach you how to keep from falling off."

"Can't I learn about your magic without dealing with demons?"

"Casting spells using sacrificial animals and graveyard dirt can only take you so far. The true power of black magic comes from harnessing demonic energy. Come on, dearie, don't be a chicken. You can do it."

She went to a cabinet and withdrew a copper bowl containing incense, placing it on the floor in the middle of the pentagram. "Obviously, no need to cut you this time. Your body is willingly volunteering your blood."

"I'm having second thoughts," I said. When I tried to stand up, my legs gave out. Ruth had cast a spell on me.

She knelt before the copper bowl, murmuring an incantation. With a wooden match, she ignited the incense, then reached into a pocket of her robe and tossed a dark powder into the flames. Grabbing my wrist, she dragged me closer to the bowl and squeezed several drops of blood onto the fire.

"Asmodeus," she called, "king of demons! I summon you to the soul to whom you are bonded."

The fire in the bowl erupted, the flames almost touching the ceiling. An icy gust of wind blew all the candles out, suppressing the incense fire to a red glow.

And in the darkness, the steps of cloven hooves approached. A towering black figure appeared, silhouetted against the faint red light. It had three heads, one of which had horns, with a pair of red, burning eyes in each. A snake-like tail whipped back and forth on the floor.

"Asmodeus is a lustful demon, but not just of carnal desire,"

Ruth said in a low voice. "He spreads the lust for power, too. That describes you, dearie. Maybe not the carnal part, though, at your age."

"I'm only forty-five. I still experience plenty of sexual desire." Why I felt the need to defend my sex life in front of a demon was beyond me.

"He is here because of your lust for magical power."

"I wouldn't call it a lust, exactly. More of a curiosity."

"Just as I am bonded to you, you are bonded to me," said a deep, raspy, gurgling voice that sent goosebumps down my arms. "Come with me."

My stomach turned to ice. "No. Please leave me alone."

A rumbling laugh came from the darkness. "Come."

My body felt yanked, as if I were wearing a parachute that had just opened. My vision went black. When I regained it, I was on my knees like before, but in a desert with an endless landscape of brown sand and slightly rolling hills beneath a crisp blue sky. I was completely alone and saw no sign of Asmodeus.

At first, I wondered if I was in the Gobi Desert and would encounter a death worm. No, a demon would have no interest in that.

This better not be like the Temptation of Christ, I thought. *I'll fail the first test the demon gives me because I could never fast for 40 days. He wouldn't need to offer to turn stones into bread; I'd just eat the stones.*

I realized that would not be the storyline when the cloud of dust appeared on the horizon and quickly drew closer. It was a car speeding across the hard-packed sand toward me. And not just any car: the fancy Italian sports car I had always coveted but never, ever thought I'd have a chance in hell—pardon the pun—of buying.

The car was a convertible, candy-apple red, and brand-new. It parked right in front of me, the powerful engine purring as if it ran on magic. At the wheel was a drop-dead gorgeous man in his early thirties wearing aviator sunglasses, with thick black hair swept back by the wind. He grinned at me with perfect white teeth. He was shirtless, and his chiseled pecs and six-pack abs glistened in the desert sun.

Have I been transported to a romance novel cover? I wondered.

The deep, raspy voice of the demon said in my mind, *Here is your first reward for using black magic and following the path of evil. Infinite money to pursue worldly pleasures. Certain famous billionaires have chosen this path, and you can too.*

This temptation seemed way over the top.

"Does the boy toy come with the car?" I asked the demon.

Absolutely. All the boy toys you could ever want. Discard the ones you tire of and buy more.

The driver tilted his shades up and gave me a come-hither smile.

"There's a flaw in your logic," I said. "My mother had pursued black magic for most of her life, and she's always struggled for money. She's barely gotten by until recently when she began extorting money from local businesspeople. Also, I've never seen her with a handsome lover."

There is no reason your life must be like your mother's, the demon replied. *Your mother never asked me for riches, but I can enable you to acquire them with ease.*

It struck me as highly unlikely that my mother wouldn't

have asked a demon for money. She was the type to ask everyone and anyone for it.

"Sorry, but I'm just not buying it. I think you're scamming me."

"Missy, let's go for a ride. As fast as you want," the sexy driver said with a suggestive wink.

"Also, I'm just not a materialistic woman," I told the demon. "As long as I can live comfortably, I don't have a lust for money. And that's a beautiful car, but I can live without it. Especially without the slab of meat behind the wheel."

"Hey! Not fair!" the driver cried.

So be it, the demon said. *I will show you other reasons to choose black magic.*

Once again, I was yanked by a powerful force and flew over the desert toward a building incongruously sitting atop a low ridge. I recognized the neoclassical architecture of the county courthouse. I soared through the open doors, down the marble-lined hallway, and landed on a wooden seat in the spectator section of a large courtroom. It was filled with people who caught their breaths as the jury filed into the room and sat down.

You investigate many crimes. Achieving justice is very important to you, is it not? the demon asked.

"It is."

I can give you magical tools to solve the most difficult mysteries. I can help you achieve justice for victims and punish the offenders. Your community will be safer because of you, and moral justice will flourish.

In the courtroom, the judge asked the jury foreperson if the jury had come to a verdict. The foreperson said they had found the defendant guilty on all counts. The families of victims sitting nearby hugged each other and sobbed with joy.

Someone behind me patted me on the back in congratulation. Detective Shortle turned around and smiled at me. Had I played a role in this case?

The defendant, standing flanked by lawyers, was not far from me, but I couldn't see who it was. The convicted felon was shrouded in a dark mist, preventing me from even identifying what gender he or she was.

Before the judge gaveled the courtroom to silence, I heard stray snippets of conversations from the spectators. The word "poisoned" was uttered several times. Then the reality sank in.

I was watching a potential future event: the trial of the Mongolian Death Worm murders.

Using black magic, with my help, you will solve this case, the demon's words rang in my head. *If you don't use it, you won't solve it. No one will. The murderer will go free.*

"You're a demon, not a soothsayer," I replied. "This scene you're showing me isn't the future, because you don't know what will happen. You're only showing me propaganda to make your case."

Don't underestimate me. I have existed for millennia. Several human religions acknowledge me. I know things far beyond human understanding.

He might be telling me the truth, and I had no way of knowing. I refused to admit it but was insecure about my convictions. Still, even if he were right, I didn't want to use black magic to investigate the case.

Asmodeus must have sensed that I wasn't convinced, and

suddenly the courthouse was gone. I sat not in a chair but on the desert sand.

A woman was crying. It seemed to be coming from behind a nearby boulder. I got to my feet and walked across the sand to the boulder. Sure enough, someone lay sleeping on the ground, wrapped in a blanket. I bent down to see her face.

It was my adoptive mother, Mabel Mindle. Her eyes were closed, her face pale, and she looked a hundred years older than when I had last seen her.

She will soon be diagnosed with stage three pancreatic cancer, the demon said. *She has only weeks to live. The best modern medical care can do nothing for her. The only thing that could save her will be black magic and my powers.*

Guilt poured into me. Mabel and my stepfather had moved to Tennessee years ago. After my stepfather passed away, I tried to convince Mabel to move back to Florida to be closer to me, but she had tired of how "whacked out" Florida had become. I wouldn't be able to make a living in the small mountain town where she lived, so I had remained in Florida. Although I visited her a couple of times a year, that wasn't enough. I know, I know.

I knelt beside her to rub her shoulders, but my hand passed right through her. She was only a phantasm conjured by the demon.

My repertoire of healing spells did not include cancer care. But I could learn more powerful magic. Angela could help me. If Mabel truly became ill, of course, and I wasn't being duped by Asmodeus.

You are misguided, the demon said. *Your magic will never be strong enough to defeat cancer. And you know it.*

"I don't believe you that black magic could heal her. The black magic I've seen has only been about harming people."

Because the sorcerers who use it are morally bad. I approve of that, of course. He made a sound that was probably laughter, but you never knew with a demon. *That doesn't mean you, a good person, couldn't use black magic for good. It's the only kind of magic that's strong enough.*

Asmodeus had known I used to be a nurse, and the instinct to heal and help people was powerful in me. I was strongly tempted to accept his offer, but my gut screamed at me not to. All along, I had known I could never willingly practice black magic, but I allowed my curiosity and lust for power to lead me astray. Along with Ruth's bullying.

That Asmodeus had tried to tempt me into embracing black magic had only made me more suspicious of it. If I needed to be fooled into choosing this path, it meant the path would lead to misery. And foolish was how I felt to have gone this far in entertaining the possibility of exploring the black arts.

It occurred to me that this elaborate charade also meant Asmodeus couldn't simply force me to accept black magic. Right? I had to agree to accept it, even if it were under false pretenses. Which gave me more agency than I had realized.

I touched my stepmother again, my hand passing through her. She looked convincingly real but was only an illusion, just like the desert landscape around me. The inklings of a plan came to me, but I pushed them from my mind so the demon wouldn't read my thoughts.

And then it was time to make a break for it.

CHAPTER 8

I HEXED YOUR LIZARD

I figured Asmodeus had the power to crush me like a grape if he wanted to. He was a demon, after all. Hell was where he was in his top form, but when he manifested himself on Earth, he was almost as formidable. Remember, demons provide the juice for much of the world's black magic. Their evil energy easily manipulates physical objects.

When Asmodeus presented my temptations to me, we weren't in a real desert on Earth. All the things I experienced were illusions created by the demon. He did a great job creating them, him being a demon, of course, but they weren't material and real. Which is what gave me hope of getting out of his clutches.

While I crouched beside the apparition of my cancer-stricken stepmother from the future, I tried to conjure some magic to free me from this theme park ride the demon had created. No luck. Missy in the desert was only an astral projection of myself. My physical body was still in Ruth's apartment, which meant I couldn't access my internal energies to cast spells.

However, Missy in the desert consisted of my consciousness and the essence of my soul, allowing me to observe, think, and feel emotions. Because I was a witch, these pieces of me provided just enough energy to analyze the magic that Asmodeus had used to bring me here.

Pretending to fuss over my mother, I probed the demon's power. The putrid, evil darkness of it made me recoil. This was ancient magic, acquired from Satan back when God created the universe, but it was nothing Godlike. The magic was corrupt, sick, and wrong. I couldn't make any sense of it.

But I recognized one key element: lust. The lore was true, then, that Asmodeus embodied the concept of lust—not just carnality, but the force of overwhelming desire in every context. He was using it on me, tempting me with my desire to achieve justice and heal the sick.

And Asmodeus himself experienced lust. Namely, the powerful desire to spend more time in the material world, even though he commanded legions of demons in hell. The only times he visited the material world were when summoned by sorcerers like Ruth. He was making me his pet project, helping to make me a powerful black-magic sorceress.

For just as he was bonded to me, I would be bonded to him, enabling him to run rampant on earth, capturing souls and gaining more power from them. I would be his ticket to doing it.

I must break the bond between us. Ruth could help me, but I doubted she would. I would have to do it myself. The first step was escaping from this illusory desert.

With all the strength my astral self could conjure, I inwardly renounced every desire he had stimulated in me. I had already turned my back on the temptation of wealth. Next, I forced myself to disavow my dedication to justice and healing. I couldn't do so permanently because those traits were an inherent part of me. Still, I could do so in the moment.

What are you doing? His voice boomed in my head. *What is happening to you?*

My emotions switched off, my mind went blank. All my senses were numbed. Every ounce of the little energy I had was focused on one thing: breaking free of this illusion.

Then, I was overcome with vertigo and the sensation of falling.

"WHAT ARE you doing back in your body?" Ruth asked, looking down at me as I writhed on the floor in terror. "It's too soon for Asmodeus to be finished with you."

When I realized I was back on Earth, my panic ceased. "Actually, my excursion has ended."

"You're not behaving the way victims—I mean, participants—of demon temptation tours usually act when they return. Don't tell me you escaped from Asmodeus?"

A thunder-like roar came from all around us, making the floor vibrate.

"I guess you did," she said. "This is not good. You were under Asmodeus's spell. You can't just leave his illusion without his permission."

"Too late," I said, getting up from the floor. "I'm taking my iguana and going home." I pushed past Ruth and marched into the hallway where Tony's cage had been placed.

"You can't just walk away from a demon who is controlling you."

"Watch me."

"Asmodeus is one of the most powerful demons. You can't defy him unless you've gone through a bond-breaking ceremony. And if he doesn't want to break from you, you're out of luck."

I picked up Tony's crate. He looked at me with frightened eyes, but wisely kept his mouth shut. "Come on, Tony. We're going home."

Ruth blocked my path. "This is unwise for you."

"You don't care about me. What's in it for you?"

"You'll be a hundred times more powerful under Asmodeus's influence. You must give us a chance to convince you to choose black magic."

"Why do you care so much? You can survive without my monthly dues."

"You're my acolyte. If you're more powerful, you'll make *me* more powerful."

"It's always about you." I pushed her aside, casting a protection spell to block whatever magic she tried to blast me with.

"Why the protection spell? I won't stop you," she said smugly. "You'll return to me willingly when you suffer the wrath of Asmodeus. He will punish you for walking out on him."

I stopped and turned to face her. "Please release me from him."

"I told you I can't break the bond if he doesn't want me to."

"How do you know he doesn't?"

"I just know these things, dearie."

"Please try anyway."

"To rise to the greatest level of black magic, you need to work with demons. If not Asmodeus, then it must be a different demon."

"I'm sorry, Ruth—"

"Saint Ruthless."

I sighed. "I'll be honest. Black magic simply isn't for me. I'm done. I'll pay your coven dues if you insist, but it's time for us to go our separate ways."

"You're not getting out of this."

A nauseating chill passed through me. It was black magic. "What spell did you cast just now?"

She cackled with delight. "I hexed your lizard again. This time, I silenced him. Until you cooperate with me, he won't be able to communicate with you in any way, even telepathically."

To be honest, that didn't seem like such a bad thing. I left the apartment without saying goodbye.

It wasn't long before I found out Tony's silence would be a huge problem.

THE CEREMONIAL WOUND in my palm opened again when I was in the shower. It was right after I got home, and I had wanted to cleanse myself of the taint of black magic and the stinky incense. Then, I had planned to relax for the rest of the afternoon. I had taken a vacation day from work, expecting it would have been filled with magic lessons. Asmodeus's temptation tour had seemed long but had taken up very little actual time. My free schedule made me feel as if I had been given an unexpected holiday.

Until my weeks-old wound began gushing blood. As it mixed with the water and ran down the drain, it reminded me of the shower scene in *Psycho*. It did not augur well. Asmodeus surely had me in his sights.

As a former nurse, I knew some basic first-aid spells and put a stop to the bleeding. But I was worried about what would come next. Would the demon attack me directly? How could I defend myself against him?

Although I didn't know if my conventional magic would be effective, I placed magical wards around the perimeter of my property in addition to the ones I normally used on the doors and windows as my burglar-alarm system. If any wards were set off by a demonic intruder, I would cast my most powerful protection spell over the house. This spell required constant feeding of energy, so I couldn't maintain it constantly.

While I was brainstorming more ideas, Tony ran into the kitchen with his splayed-out lizard legs moving in a blur.

"Are you okay?" I asked.

He shook his head in the negative, repeatedly opening and closing his mouth as he struggled to talk.

"Sorry, Tony. I'll try to break Ruth's hex on you, but my priority is defending myself against Asmodeus."

Tony stared at me in anguish as his tail whipped back and forth.

"Do you have any advice on how to stop a demon?" I asked.

He did a series of lizard pushups—gestures lizards use in courtship and to display dominance. I wasn't sure if this was his way of nodding yes or trying to look sexy.

"Do you have something important to tell me?"

He repeated the movements while opening and closing his mouth.

"Can you write?" I placed a pad and pen in front of him. He obviously knew how to talk, but after all these years with him, I didn't know if he could write. He would often sit on my shoulder when I studied grimoires to learn new spells, so I knew he could read. But could the little bugger compose anything?

He gripped the pen with his right claw—which was easy for him, because iguanas naturally grip tree branches—but struggled to write with it. No one had bothered to teach penmanship to the lizard. He managed to scrawl a short vertical line and a diagonal one before giving up in frustration.

"I have an idea," I said. "I'll be right back."

In the back of my bedroom closet, hidden on the top shelf, was an old Ouija board I had saved since childhood. It had been my very first connection to the spirit world, before I realized I had been born with the magic gene.

I put the board on the kitchen floor in front of Tony. He nodded in recognition, which demonstrated his long experience as a witch's familiar. I pushed the heart-shaped wooden planchette close to his front legs. His right claw grasped it and slid it across the Ouija board's painted alphabet, stopping on one letter at a time. I wrote them down:

M-a-t-e-o

"You want Don Mateo?" I asked.

Tony nodded in his push-up fashion. I hadn't thought of summoning my resident ghost, but it made sense because they had known each other for centuries, from back when the wizard lived. Perhaps his spirit could communicate with the hexed iguana better than I could.

I positioned myself beside Don Mateo's favorite place in the material world: my lingerie drawer. Don't ask me why, but the guy obviously had a kinky side when he was alive four hundred years ago.

"Don Mateo," I called out. "Please come. Tony and I need your help."

Several minutes passed, but he didn't appear. I removed a pair of red panties from the drawer and waved them like a flag. "Don Mateo? Please come."

The cats, who had been napping atop the bed, suddenly bolted. They had sensed the supernatural energy even before I had.

The red panties were yanked from my hand. Suspended in the air, they ballooned, as if inflated with air. And then, the bearded head of Don Mateo appeared, wearing the panties like a surgical cap. The rest of him materialized soon afterwards.

"How can I be of assistance, M'lady?" he asked with an extravagant bow.

"Tony has been hexed by Ruth, and he can't communicate. I think he believes you can help him."

"I will certainly try."

The light clicking of lizard claws approached across the hardwood floor, and Tony entered the bedroom. It was odd not to hear the sarcastic comments that usually came with his arrival.

"Antonio, my old friend," Don Mateo said. "I'm here to be your interpreter. Allow me to read your thoughts."

The room was filled with silence, followed by an exasperated grunt from the ghost. "I can't seem to get through."

"Ruth told me that he and I couldn't use telepathy to communicate. What are you using?"

"As a ghost, I can't use telepathy. I'm using a high-level spiritual channel that should connect with him because he's a familiar who has been reincarnated several times. I can sense that he's upset about his condition and fearful of some impending danger. But no words came forth from him."

"You're frightened of something?" I asked Tony.

He nodded.

"Let me get the Ouija board." I hurried to the kitchen and brought it to the bedroom. "Tell us what you're frightened of?"

The iguana moved the planchette rapidly over the alphabet portion of the board, pausing it on certain letters that I wrote down.

What I wrote was: *Ruth will kill you.*

Don Mateo and I both gasped.

CHAPTER 9

RATTING OUT RUTH

I sat across a conference table from Detective Shortle at the Jellyfish Beach Police Department. The room in the small headquarters was used for interviews, interrogations, administrative meetings, and, apparently, birthday parties. An abandoned, stale-looking piece of cake sat on a paper plate at the far end of the table. A fat fly dive-bombed it.

"It was the first question you asked me when you arrived at the house after Mrs. Fusseldink died," I said. "You asked if black-magic witchcraft was responsible. Well, the more I think about it, the more I believe that was the case. And the more I'm certain that the sorceress who did it was Ruth Bent."

"Why hadn't you told me this before?" she asked me.

"Well, I told you she was demanding protection money from the downtown merchants."

"Those I spoke to denied it."

"They were too frightened of her to confirm it. Look," I said, "Ruth Bent, aka Ophelia Lawthorne, is my birth mother. Even though we're not close, it's difficult for me to rat her out. But I know she was behind the desecrations at the houses of worship you investigated. And the fiasco at the charity gala in the hotel, with the bats and the water turning into blood? Definitely her."

Shortle took notes. "I've spoken to her once in the past. She was not cooperative."

"I'm not surprised."

"She was pretty nasty, in fact."

"Sounds like Ruth, all right. And I think she might be the poisoner you're looking for."

Did I truly believe Ruth was the murderer of Mrs. Fusseldink and the jogger on the beach? I didn't know of any connection between them, but Ruth certainly had black-magic spells that could kill people in a manner similar to the unusual venom. I reminded myself of this to tamp down the guilt I felt for falsely accusing her when I knew that the death worm was the most likely cause of their deaths.

How could I feel guilty for a mother who had tried to kill me in the past and wouldn't hesitate to do so again? According to Tony, she was, in fact, planning to kill me. If you're wondering how my iguana would know that, trust me. Tony's spirit has been on this earth for centuries, and he just knew stuff, especially if it involved the supernatural.

Even if my witch's familiar was mistaken, it was time to resist Ruth. I was tired of all her bullying and terrorizing. Worst of all, she had made me the target of a demon—a most powerful one. She had me up against the wall. And I had no way of fighting back except to get the police on my side. The police couldn't help me with Asmodeus, but they would put Ruth on the defensive as she was investigated for black-magic vandalism. It was a delaying tactic to get her off my back.

In the end, Shortle wouldn't find evidence tying Ruth to the murders. But if the detective was thorough, she would uncover how extensive Ruth's crime network was and hopefully break up the coven. Shortle had been more open-minded about the supernatural than most cops, but even if she didn't believe the coven practiced real magic, she would realize it was a cult that exploited its vulnerable members.

"I also have it on good authority that Ruth Bent is planning to kill me," I added.

"Who told you that?"

"Um, a friend."

"You're playing games with me. I doubt Bent was the poisoner," Shortle said. She gave a self-satisfied smile, her face seemingly pulled backward by her tight ponytail. "We've been working on a very promising lead."

"Do tell."

"You already know about him."

"The poisoner who's out of prison on parole?"

"Yes. Convicted of murdering four people decades ago, women who were around the same age and physical profile as the most recent victims. He happens to be staying with his family in Jellyfish Beach."

"That's the best lead you've got?" I tried to keep the mockery out of my voice but failed. "I looked him up on the internet. He killed two wives and two girlfriends—one after the other—by slipping potassium cyanide into their protein shakes. That's a completely different MO than killing a cryptozoologist's wife in her bedroom and a jogger on the beach with burns on their faces. Does he have any connections to the victims?"

"We're following up on that."

"And he went from slipping cyanide into drinks to spraying people with an exotic venom never seen before?"

"He has evolved to a new chapter in his life as a poisoner. As I mentioned before, venom can be milked from snakes. The Medical Examiner said the venom found on the victims came from a viper."

"She told me it *resembled* viper venom but couldn't be identified as coming from a known species."

Shortle frowned. "You seem to enjoy raining on my parade."

"That's not true."

"Everyone agrees that the cause of death could not be the venomous worm the victim's husband was searching for in Mongolia."

I didn't agree but kept my mouth shut.

"That worm is nothing but a legendary creature with no evidence that it exists," Shortle continued. "Definitely no evidence of it where the victims were found. I might as well suspect the Loch Ness Monster. And now you're accusing Ruth Bent of murdering the victims with black magic. There is not a single homicide-investigation textbook that mentions black magic as a cause of death."

"It didn't have to be magic itself. She could have used a deadly potion she created."

Shortle shook her head. "We have an actual convicted poisoner in our town. He must be ruled out as a suspect before I go chasing your cockamamie theories."

"Okay," I said, rising from my chair. "You really ought to

investigate the extortion of our local merchants. Talk to Fred Furman. Or any of the others."

Detective Marty Glasbag entered the room. The portly, middle-aged man ignored me and whispered into Shortle's ear. She jumped out of her seat.

"You know the way out, Mindle." She barely glanced at me before leaving the room.

Glasbag noticed the abandoned piece of cake at the end of the table. He quickly snatched it and hurried out the door as if he didn't know I was watching.

Something was up, and no one was going to tell a civilian like me. So, I called Matt, who was always glued to his police-band radio.

"I haven't heard anything ominous," Matt replied. "The only thing was a medical emergency at the country club golf course. Probably a heart attack. Nothing remarkable about that in a town like this with so many old people."

My mind raced. "You know what they have at all golf courses? Sand traps."

"The proper name is bunkers."

"Don't mansplain. I'll meet you there ASAP."

The Jellyfish Beach Golf and Tennis Club sprawled across prime real estate near the oceanfront. Parts of the golf course were right behind the sand dunes, offering golfers spectacular views of the surf. The sixteenth hole, in particular, had a fairway running parallel to the shore and a green perched high enough to provide picture-perfect putting.

The green was also surrounded by large sand traps. Sorry, bunkers. A body lay covered with a tarp on the sand, surrounded by crime-scene investigators. You don't need CSI when someone drops dead from a heart attack, so it appeared my hunch about the worm had been correct.

In the rough outside the bunkers, Detectives Glasbag and Shortle held an animated conversation with Matt, who had beaten me to the scene. As I approached, I heard Matt demand the names of the players who had witnessed the death of a member of their foursome.

"No media yet," Glasbag told him.

"We need to conduct additional interviews with them at the station," Shortle explained. She glanced at me with irritation when I walked up to the detectives.

"Did the poisoner use a spray bottle filled with venom?" I asked sarcastically.

She gave me an angry smile. "No. Because the victim wasn't poisoned." Her tone was as condescending as possible.

"What happened? It wasn't a heart attack, was it?"

"No comment."

"The other players saw what happened, right?"

"I'll tell you one thing," Shortle said with a sneer. "They didn't see an elderly black-magic sorceress."

I knew they hadn't, but I was disappointed that my attempt to use Ruth as a red herring had failed already.

"Can't you speculate about the cause of death?" Matt asked the detectives.

"We need the ME for that," Shortle replied.

"Lightning," Glasbag blurted out. "The victim was struck by lightning."

Shortle elbowed him in the ribs.

"Odd for such a sunny day," Matt said. "No clouds at all in the sky."

"You know how thunderstorm cells can pop up out of nowhere this time of year," Glasbag replied.

Lightning strike meant electrocution. Did that mean the worm did it? After all, part of its legend was the ability to shock creatures with its tail.

"Ruth Bent knows more than one spell that conjures lightning bolts," I said. Shortle ignored me. She and Glasbag turned their backs to us and shared their great wisdom with each other.

Their ignoring me turned out to be a benefit. I noticed three male golfers standing on the golf cart path. Officer Bird kept an eye on them. They must be the surviving members of the foursome, waiting for the detectives to interview them. I wandered over.

"Gentlemen," I said. "I'm so sorry for your loss. Detective Glasbag said your friend was struck by lightning?"

"Lightning? Ha!" said a man with a crew cut and an unlit cigar in his mouth. "There wasn't any lightning."

"You're not supposed to be here, Missy," Bird told me. The officer was young and pretty, with short hair and a pert nose. She didn't intimidate me in the slightest.

"Go on, please," I said to the golfers.

"Charlie was attacked by a freaking snake," said a tall, thin fellow. "Weird-looking thing. It killed him."

"It looked like the snake electrocuted him," said the cigar guy. "I saw a flash of light going up the shaft of Charlie's sand wedge, and after he went down, there was a burnt smell. He was in that bunker over there when the snake came out of the sand and went after him."

"What color was the snake?"

"Light red with dark red blotches."

That matched the description I'd read of the Mongolian Death Worm.

"What happened to the snake after it electrocuted your friend?"

"It burrowed into the sand and disappeared."

The death worm had obviously migrated to the sand trap—sorry, bunker—from the adjacent beach. Unless it had already replicated itself, and this was one of its offspring. No, I simply couldn't believe a baby could grow *that* fast.

I returned to the green and joined Matt, who was talking on his phone. When he was finished, I told him what I had learned.

"Awesome work, Missy!"

Then I mentioned my speculation about the worm migrating or reproducing.

"Let's hope this wasn't a baby worm and that they don't grow that quickly," he said. "Can you ask the ickologist you met, Dr. Hooey, about it?"

"Yeah. But I'm afraid of what his answer will be."

The sound of thumping came from the bunker. Glasbag stomped back and forth across the sand. "There are no burrows under here," he said to Shortle, unaware that we were listening. "Snakes don't make their own burrows; they use ones made by other creatures, like the gopher tortoise."

I turned to Matt. "Glasbag shouldn't be making vibrations like that if a worm is around. Should I tell him?"

"Then you'd have to explain how you know."

"I can't let him get hurt."

Too late. A high-pitched shriek came from the bunker, a

scream several octaves higher than a fat guy like Glasbag should have been capable of.

A death worm oozed from the sand and raised its head like a cobra facing Glasbag.

"Duck!" I yelled.

He did duck, just as a stream of amber liquid shot from the creature's mouth. His action saved him from getting the full blast of venom in his face, but his bald forehead was struck; blisters quickly appeared, and yellow blotches spread. The detective dropped to his knees in the sand.

"Wow, that hurts," he said with a huge grin. "Gimme some more!"

A gunshot rang out, and a tiny geyser of sand erupted beside the worm. The creature formed an upside-down U, then its head disappeared beneath the sand, followed by the rest of its body. The body was fatter and shorter than a snake's, resembling a kielbasa.

Shortle continued to shoot at the sand while Glasbag fell onto his back, moving his arms and legs like he was doing the backstroke in a swimming pool. He giggled as the euphoric effects of the venom overcame him. If Shortle hadn't frightened the death worm away, it surely would have sprayed more venom on Glasbag and ended his life.

However, if Shortle continued shooting, she might hit Glasbag. She finally stopped.

But more gunshots filled the air as a panicked male officer fired rounds into the sand. His fear and frenzied shooting caused Shortle to shoot again until her clip emptied. A third cop joined in, firing wildly at nothing. Now the bunker was more of a lead trap than a sand trap. Finally, everyone calmed down and put their guns away. I shook my head in disbelief at the trigger-happy cops.

"Gimme more juice!" Glasbag said in a drunken voice.

"What the heck was that thing?" Shortle asked of no one in particular.

"I believe we're the first Americans to see a Mongolian Death Worm and survive," I replied. "It's time to retire your theory of the mad poisoner."

She said nothing, still stunned by what she had seen.

As a rule, I never wanted the police involved in supernatural affairs. Often, it turned out that humans were responsible for the murders the Society and I worried had been committed by monsters. Every once in a while, a monster was the guilty party. This was one of those instances, and there was no way to make the police unsee what they had witnessed. I needed to decide whether I would work with them to find out who had released the worm into our community.

"The convicted poisoner obviously used a Mongolian Death Worm as his murder weapon," Shortle said.

I shook my head again. Never mind. Let the police try to solve this on their own. Matt and I would continue to investigate Milo until we had enough evidence to satisfy the Cryptids Society's justice department.

And we had to find the errant worm, or worms, before anyone else died.

CHAPTER 10

DEVOTED TO THE DEATH WORM

Milo Fusseldink opened his apartment door and eyed us warily. He had a book tucked under one arm, something about Bigfoot, and a fried-chicken drumstick in his other hand. A speck of chicken hung in his unruly white beard. His shirt was untucked and had a large stain where it covered his potbelly. Milo's time living apart from his wife had apparently turned him into the model of a slovenly bachelor.

"What do you want?" he demanded.

Matt smiled. "I'm Matt Rosen with *The Jellyfish Beach Journal*."

Milo's eyes narrowed with suspicion.

"I'm Missy Mindle with the Friends of Cryptids Society of the Americas."

His expression changed to one of curiosity. "Are you a cryptozoologist?"

"I'm a field worker for the Society. I catalog and monitor cryptids and supernatural creatures."

This sparked his interest. "Is it true, then? A Mongolian Death Worm is in the US?"

I hadn't expected him to go there right away. In my pocket was a small bag of the powder I used for my truth spell, because I had expected him to offer nothing but denial.

"You tell us," I replied.

"Why weren't you at your wife's funeral?" Matt asked in an aggressive tone to throw our subject off balance.

Milo hung his head in shame. "Because no one informed me of her death. I only learned of it when I saw the death notice in the newspaper the day of the funeral, too late to attend. I'm often negligent in keeping up with the news. There are so many scientific journals to read."

"Where were you on the day she died?"

"On the thirteenth? That's the date the death notice gave."

"Yes. Where were you?"

"Who are you to be asking me these questions?"

"I'm a reporter who can ruin your reputation if you don't cooperate."

"Okay," Milo said in a huff. "I was in the hospital. Heart issues."

"Which hospital?"

"Jellyfish Beach Memorial."

"What about the days before her death?"

"I was in the hospital for two weeks before her death."

This meant it was unlikely he had planted the worm. Unlikely, but not impossible. Dr. Hooey had said the creature could survive for long periods of time without sustenance, so Milo still could have placed the worm in his house earlier.

"Why did you ask us about the death worm?" I demanded. "The death notice said nothing about the cause of death."

"I read a newspaper article about the death of my wife and a jogger on the beach. It contained forensic details that indicated the *allghoi khorkhoi* might be responsible."

"That was my article," Matt said with a proud, idiotic smile.

"How did the death worm get to America?" I asked.

"Come in, come in," Milo said. "I'll tell you everything I know."

Maybe if I were lucky, I wouldn't need my truth spell after all.

Matt and I followed Milo inside and pretended that we had never been in the cluttered apartment before. The cryptozoologist headed straight for a filing cabinet beside his messy desk, placed the half-eaten drumstick on it, and pulled folders from the top drawer. Matt and I stood around staring at the various specimens and mementos that covered the wall and every surface that didn't have books or papers on it.

There were plenty I hadn't noticed during our first, rushed visit here. A framed color photo showed Milo and another man his age standing above an unconscious bear-like creature lying on the forest floor with a tranquilizer dart sticking out of its shoulder. It was large and furless, with reptilian skin and large, alien-like eyes.

"A chupacabra!" I exclaimed. "But you wrote a book debunking the creature's existence."

Milo stopped what he was doing and glanced at the photo. "The book merely debunked a crop of stories about chupacabras and supposed witnesses when they gained worldwide attention. We were critical of the people peddling false narratives to profit from them. Both Dr. Levings and I had contact with the species, as you can see from that photo."

"But I thought the book almost got you guys kicked out of the cryptozoology world."

"Our editors botched the job and made the book seem biased. Anyone who read it carefully, though, would know that we were certain the chupacabra existed. Too bad that photo was taken after the book was published. I'm saving it for something special."

"Didn't you have a falling out with Dr. Levings over the book?" Matt asked.

Milo looked at him strangely. "Over many things, but not *that* book. A different book. Have you been speaking with someone from his staff?"

"Zora Marchovsky," Matt replied.

"You should have spoken to me first, not any of Levings's people."

"We didn't know you were in Florida, much less alive. You went missing, remember?"

Milo chuckled. "True. You've got me there."

"How long have you been here?"

"I returned a few weeks ago. Before I went to the hospital."

"Why did you slip away from your desert camp without telling anyone?" I asked.

"Levings and I were quarreling bitterly, and I figured he wouldn't miss me. I wanted to come home and work with no one bothering me, especially my wife. We found the worm's molted skin, a true triumph, and I didn't believe the expedition would accomplish anything more."

"Sounds like you were faking your death," Matt said.

"Nonsense," Milo said, clearly annoyed.

"Tell us about your research on the death worm," Matt said, trying to get back into the scientist's good graces.

Milo pointed to one of the folders he had pulled from the filing cabinet, a particularly thick one. "I have a nearly completed manuscript of a book about the Mongolian Death Worm, but I still have never seen one. All I have is a skin from a worm. I wanted to capture a living specimen and introduce it to the world. This remarkable creature deserves attention and study. It is incredibly deadly but has eluded humans throughout our entire existence. No wonder it has become such a legend. And it has more weaponry than its venom. The worm is one of the few electrogenic creatures that's not a fish, and it's rumored to be more powerful than electric eels."

"Yes. Much more powerful. It can kill a human," I said. "If you see on the news a story about a golfer struck by lightning, he was actually electrocuted by a death worm."

"Brilliant!" Milo was exuberant. "I must examine its electric organs. And most of all, I want a sample of its venom. My hypothesis is that it's the most toxic venom of any creature on Earth. And I believe it has the potential to lead to new life-saving drugs for human beings. If only I could capture the worm."

"Um, so you're not the one who brought a worm to the US?" Matt asked.

"No, Levings must have done so. Who else could have

found one and brought it here? And the only reason he kept it secret was that he intended to use it to kill Claire."

"Why would he kill your wife?" Matt asked.

Milo paused. My instinct told me it was time for the truth spell. I sidled up to Milo and absently leafed through the photos and sketches in an open folder on his desk. In reality, I was focusing all my energies on casting the spell. At the right moment, I took a pinch of powder from the baggie in my pocket and sprinkled it on Milo's shoes while he was staring at Matt.

"Do you believe Dr. Levings killed your wife?" Matt asked again.

"To be honest, I'm not certain." He had a glassy look in his eyes, which meant the spell had kicked in and he was, in fact, being honest. "I suspected they were having an affair or had one in the past. He's unmarried, by the way. I don't know why he would feel the need to murder Claire, however."

With the spell working, it was time for me to take over the questioning to maintain my magical connection with him. "What about you, Dr. Fusseldink? Did *you* kill Claire?"

"Why would I do that?" He appeared to be struggling against the spell-induced urge to be honest and unburden himself.

I pressed harder. "You were estranged from her, and she was having an affair with your rival. She had a large inheritance from her family. Possibly life insurance, too. All that money could fund your research indefinitely."

He remained silent. Yes, he was struggling against the truth spell, but he also seemed befuddled by our line of questioning. "You're not the police. Why would you ask me such a thing?"

"Did you kill her?"

"The very idea of that is absurd."

"Did you capture a death worm and bring it back to America?"

He laughed nervously. "Of course not. Capturing one is my life's goal, and I would have trumpeted it to the heavens had I succeeded. Why are you asking me so many questions?"

"We need to learn who set the worm free in your home and why. Also, witnesses say a woman who resembled Dr. Levings's research assistant, Zora Marchovsky, was seen coming and going from your apartment. Was that her?"

"I don't know. I haven't seen her since Mongolia. Why would she visit my apartment?"

"That's what I want to know. Has she ever visited you here before?"

"Never. She must have broken in."

I didn't want to reveal that we'd seen the photo he took of her leaving Levings's tent, but I needed to ask about it. "Is she unnaturally close to Dr. Levings?"

"Unnaturally?"

"More than an assistant. His lover, maybe?"

"I've wondered that myself. She seems involved in his life in a greater role than as a researcher. He treats her like a personal servant. But also like a friend. One shouldn't become so close to one's research assistant."

Milo's eyes were becoming more lucid, which meant the truth spell was wearing off. My time for questioning was running out.

"Dr. Fusseldink, faking your disappearance in the Gobi Desert was a rather extreme way to get privacy to do your work," I said. "You had already separated from your wife. Why did you put her through the mental anguish of not knowing your fate?"

"I assure you she couldn't care less about what happened to me. No one does, except for students and other researchers who want something from me."

"That's not true. Your wife asked me to help find you."

"*You?* How could you find me?"

"Long story for another time. Anyway, wouldn't being perceived as missing harm your career?"

"On the contrary." He smiled like a devil. "The publicity was invaluable. The cryptozoology community loves secrets and conspiracies. And I plan to surface soon when I publish my new book."

"About what?"

He picked up the folder containing his manuscript. "It will prove the Mongolian Death Worm exists, and I will take sole credit for proving so. Furthermore, it will prove that Levings is a fraud and will completely discredit him."

"My last questions are about him." I had to hurry; the spell was almost gone. "Would Dr. Levings want to kill you?"

Milo snorted. "Heavens, yes."

"Really?" My question had been a random long shot.

"Ever since our friendship and professional partnership soured, he hated me. The feeling was mutual, to be honest. In a field as small as ours, there's only enough room for one superstar, and that's me." His face fell. "Well, it *was* me before I began the slide into irrelevance. Levings delighted in that and wanted me out of the picture so he could shine in my place. We almost came to blows in the Gobi Desert before I came home."

"If Dr. Levings found the worm, it would bring him the

fame he wanted, right? Would he waste the opportunity by using the worm to kill Claire? Or you?"

"Ah, you're thinking the worm was meant for me?"

"It was in your dresser drawer."

He scratched his beard in thought, dislodging the piece of chicken in it. "Yes, he could have planted the worm to kill me. Afterward, he could present the creature to the world. Apparently, he made an enormous error and allowed the worm to escape."

"He didn't plan on other people, like me, being in the house, preventing him from retrieving the worm in time."

"You were there when she died? You hadn't told me that. Was her death painful?" The spell was gone, and Milo's sincerity was difficult to assess.

"She passed away with a smile on her face," I said, telling the truth.

I DROVE MATT HOME, and we discussed what we had learned.

"I don't think Milo is completely off the hook," Matt said. "He kind of hedged when you asked him if he killed his wife. But Levings is definitely a suspect in my eyes."

"We need to speak with him, even if he refused to meet us before. Can we get Zora to convince him to?"

"We need leverage of some sort."

"Hmm. We have one advantage," I said as I pulled up in front of Matt's bungalow. "You, Mr. Aggressive Reporter, could imply that you suspect Levings planted the worm and is responsible for Claire's death. And if he won't talk to us, you'll go to the police."

"That kind of behavior isn't ethical for a journalist."

"I'm bonded to a demon. Ethics are a bit too quaint for me now. Besides, we must find out who put the worm in the Fusseldink home before the police do, in order to satisfy the Society's justice department."

Matt laughed. "The police are so out of their league, I wouldn't worry about them."

Turns out Matt was wrong. When I returned home, Shortle was sitting in her car in front of my house, waiting for me.

CHAPTER 11
BITTER RIVALS

I drove past Shortle's car, parked in my driveway, and walked to the front door, ignoring her. She caught up to me after I disabled the magical wards and was slipping my key in.

"I need you to tell me what you learned about Milo Fusseldink," she said.

I didn't open the door. "Why?"

"I'm asking you to cooperate with our investigation."

"Does this mean you've finally given up on your paroled poisoner theory?"

"Yeah. We will speak of that no more. But I have to say, everyone assumed Fusseldink was rotting away in the sands of the Gobi Desert. He would have been the first person I interrogated if I had known he was here in Florida."

"I need to feed my cats and iguana," I said, opening the door.

"I'm not stopping you." She followed me inside. "You don't have an alarm system?"

"Not a conventional one."

She watched me turn on the lights and grab cans of cat food from the kitchen pantry. "How long have you known Fusseldink was here?"

"You followed me to his apartment, didn't you?"

"Yes. And then I had the landlord confirm he lived there and that his rent payments were up to date. You saved me a lot of trouble."

"Glad I could be of service." I plopped minced wet food into two cat bowls and filled a third bowl with romaine, bok choy, and kale.

"Kale?" Shortle made a face.

"My iguana likes it."

"At least somebody does. Look, Mindle, don't make me beg you for information. Do you think Fusseldink was responsible for his wife's death?"

I didn't answer until I had delivered the food to my babies. The cats were wary of an unfamiliar person in the house. Tony appeared to be as well, but couldn't speak, so I didn't worry about Shortle overhearing him and wondering who the man in the garage with the New York accent was.

When I returned to the kitchen, I found Shortle seated at the table, waiting with an open notebook. It didn't seem like I'd be rid of her soon.

"I don't think Milo was behind his wife's death," I said, putting a kettle on the stove. "How do you take your tea?"

"None for me, thanks. Why don't you think Milo did it?"

"He didn't sound like he wanted to get rid of his wife, only to avoid her. Maybe he was lying to me. Who knows? But I'll tell you one thing: if Milo had a death worm in his possession, he would have used it to become famous, not to kill someone. There are many ways to commit murder, but the only way for a crypto-zoologist to become world famous is by producing one of the most famous cryptids. And I honestly believe he didn't find one."

Shortle slapped the cover of her notebook shut and stood. "Thank you for your help, as little as it was. I'll go talk to him myself."

We said goodbye, and I considered the flaw in my logic. You see, I needed to talk to a different cryptozoologist who wanted to be famous, who I suspected used his path to fame as a murder weapon instead.

"I PLAYED DIRTY LIKE YOU WANTED," Matt said as he drove his truck on the interstate highway across the Everglades. "I spoke to the research assistant and made innuendos about Levings's guilt in planting the worm. She convinced Levings to meet with us to put an end to our suspicions. But I don't like working this way. He's going to be hostile."

"I didn't say you had to do it this way," I replied, staring at the unending stretch of green wetlands to my right. "But Levings wouldn't speak with us before. You've done plenty of hostile interviews in your career. Not every person you write about is a woman in a nursing home celebrating her hundredth birthday, even in this town."

"Did you bring your ground-up eye of newt, or whatever it is you use for your truth spell?"

"It's an artisanal powder made with natural ingredients and no organs. The powder is less important than the magic that powers this spell. And, as you know, it works no matter how hostile the targets are."

I didn't add that the powder is the weak link of the spell I had learned from a medieval grimoire. You could say the spell was old-school compared to my more powerful ones that didn't require powders, potions, amulets, or charms. With magic, tradition mattered more than practicality.

The reason the powder was the weak link of my truth spell was that it needed to be sprinkled on the feet, or just underfoot, of the subject. That was easy when they were seated with you at a table, their legs hidden, and you could do the sprinkling unseen. Such wasn't the case when we sat in easy chairs in Dr. Levings's office, the professor's legs and feet fully visible across from us.

Another complicating factor for this interview was Zora's insistence on being there. Matt had grumbled that it was easier for subjects to clam up when they had moral support behind them.

"Yes, Milo found a molted skin, but that was the closest any of us came to finding a Mongolian Death Worm," Levings said in a stilted, academic voice.

Levings was tall, and his expensive gray suit didn't hide his lankiness. The arrogant man resembled the aristocratic British explorers of the nineteenth century, contrasting with Milo, who was a grubby, enthusiastic type, more in the vein of a computer hacker than a researcher.

"Have you tested the DNA of the skin?" Matt asked.

"No, because it went missing with Milo. He apparently took it with him, or his abductors did."

"Do you believe Milo is alive?" I asked, keeping Milo's location secret according to plan.

Levings stroked his long chin. "I couldn't care less. We had a falling out, you see. I wanted nothing more to do with that charlatan."

"I think he's alive," Zora said, her Eastern European accent loud and grating. "During the expedition, we interviewed a group of desert nomads who claimed to have seen death worms. I believe Milo bought a worm from them and took it home to kill his wife."

Levings remained stone-faced. He must have been familiar with her theory.

"Why would he kill her?" Matt asked Zora.

"The usual reasons. Insurance money. I heard she also came from money. Or he could have had a woman on the side."

Milo didn't seem like the type to have a mistress. Although I wondered why someone matching Zora's description had been seen at Milo's place in the past. Did she know he had returned?

"Dr. Levings, how well did you know Claire Fusseldink?" Matt asked.

The professor tried to keep up his air of aristocratic nonchalance, but his face turned as red as a beet. "Barely."

Zora turned angrily to Matt. "You were hinting at something incriminating when you demanded this interview. Are you trying to damage Dr. Levings's reputation?"

"I'm not trying to do anything but uncover the truth. Dr. Levings, did you have an affair with Mrs. Fusseldink?"

As a nurse, I was concerned Levings was going to have a stroke or heart attack, his face turning an even darker red, and his entire body trembling with rage. As a witch detective, I was frustrated I couldn't sprinkle my truth-spell powder on his feet without being caught.

"You are being absurd!" Levings was breathless, hyperventilating.

"Are you angry because Claire broke off the affair?" Matt kept going like a pit bull. "The humiliation of being dumped has led many men to murder. Doing it with a death worm would send such a powerful message to Milo, if he's still alive. It might also incriminate him. But if you admit to us about the affair, it will make you appear innocent."

All Levings could utter was a rage-filled gurgle.

I knew he wouldn't give an honest answer, so I changed the subject. "Did you know that Milo was writing a book?"

Levings took a deep breath to calm himself. "When you're a scientist, you must always be writing something. Whether it's a piece for an academic journal or a book." His eyes grew wider. "You say a book? About what? Surely not about the death worm?"

"Yes, it is."

"How do you know this?"

"We contacted his publisher," I lied, watching Levings's reactions carefully.

"Finding the molted skin justifies an entire book?"

Levings appeared not to know about the new book, but I couldn't tell if it was an act. If I told him the new book would attempt to prove the creature did, in fact, exist, and that the text would slander him, Levings would surely suffer a brain aneurysm. It could even spur him to seek revenge. Perhaps if he had known about the book, it could have led him to plant a worm in Milo's dresser. I decided to say no more about it.

"Dr. Levings," Matt said in a calm, measured tone. "Would you say that Milo has become more of a rival than a partner?"

"He was always both to me. Now, I consider him unworthy of my attention. He's a failed rival. His career is spiraling into irrelevance. And he's missing in the Gobi Desert."

"Oh, you didn't know that he's actually here in America?"

I studied Levings's face, but he showed no reaction to Matt's revelation. Neither did Zora.

"Who cares?" Levings replied.

"Then you would have no wish to kill him, right?"

Levings's face regained its purple shade. "Don't be absurd. Scientists don't kill one another."

"What if a woman were involved?"

"We're done here," Zora said loudly, rising from her chair. "I'll show you the way out."

"Keep an eye on the professor," I told her as she pushed us out the door. "He should see a doctor for his high blood pressure."

Matt and I hurried to the truck, as if we worried Levings would come after us with a machete. I felt better once we were on the road.

"That's why I avoid hostile interviews," Matt said.

"Sure, there was nothing you could quote for a newspaper story, but the vibes told me we needed to investigate Levings further. I do think he had an affair with Claire."

"I wish you could have cast your truth spell."

"Me too. My witchcraft couldn't help us, but I'm hoping

your journalistic skills can. There must be witnesses who can confirm whether there was an affair."

"Zora probably could. But she won't, not after the hostile interview."

"I bet you can find someone else."

Matt sighed. "That's a lot of work."

"Nothing about this case has been easy." I wanted to add that nothing in my life has been easy lately, but no one likes a complainer.

"Wow, is that a gator crossing the highway up ahead?" Matt asked. "Bet that happens a lot around here."

The highway stretched across the labyrinth of creeks, channels, ponds, grasslands, and tree hammocks of the Everglades. In fact, running right next to our stretch of roadway was a canal. A fence was supposed to keep the wildlife from entering the highway, but it hadn't stopped the gator strolling nonchalantly into our lane. It stopped and turned its head to look at us.

Except it wasn't really a gator.

Matt slowed the truck. "What the heck?" He glanced at his side mirrors, preparing to change lanes.

The gator transformed before our eyes, growing immensely bigger and rising on two legs with three heads. My left palm burned and grew wet with warm blood.

"Asmodeus," I whispered.

CHAPTER 12

DEMONIC TRAFFIC HAZARD

Because of the heavy traffic, we couldn't change lanes. Matt braked hard before reaching the demon, and we both tensed, afraid of being rear-ended by a vehicle. Asmodeus had grown to at least thirty feet tall, with a human head in the center and those of a bull and a goat on either side. The human mouth sprayed fire. Dragon wings on the demon's back flapped, and a snake-like tail whipped back and forth. One of its rooster-like legs kicked a passing minivan and sent it off the road.

I was paralyzed with fear but forced myself to cast a protection spell around Matt and me, including the truck. There was no guarantee it would stop a powerful demon from crushing us to a pulp.

"Who? What?" Matt's voice quavered with terror.

"He's a demon named Asmodeus. I'm afraid this is all my fault. I refused the demon's temptations for me to become evil. My bad."

Aside from the unfortunate minivan, traffic whizzed past the hulking creature as if he weren't there. Maybe only Matt and I could see him. A horn blared behind us. Matt stepped on the gas and pulled into the adjoining lane, attempting to drive around the demon.

Not so fast. The truck, within its protective bubble, rose into the air as the demon lifted it in one hand. He raised us to eye level—or, I should say, multiple-eyes level. The human eyes of its middle head studied us like King Kong gazing upon Fay Wray in his fist. The other heads glared at us with animalistic fury.

Matt whimpered.

I rolled down my window and shouted, "Asmodeus! Let my friend go. He committed no offense against you."

The demon shook the car like a kid checking how much candy was left in the box.

"I'm calling nine-one-one," Matt said.

"The Florida Highway Patrol can't do anything to stop Asmodeus. Not even with a traffic ticket."

I needed to fight back with magic. Though my power was pathetically weak compared to the demon's, there must be some spell in my repertoire that could help us.

Tires screeched, followed by the crunch of metallic impact below us. Asmodeus held our vehicle at a slight angle that allowed me to see the accident. An SUV had slammed into the demon's gigantic rooster legs. This meant that though the demon was probably invisible to the other cars on the highway, it was present in material form, in a physical body, as fantastical as it might be.

A car crashed into the rear of the disabled SUV. The nurse in me wanted to escape Matt's truck and drop to the ground so I could help the crash victims. But the witch in me sensed an opportunity. Because being bound to a demon enhanced my sense of smell.

I smelled blood. Not just the bleeding in my palm, but a small amount of blood from an accident victim below us—a trickle from a bloody nose caused by the deployment of an airbag. There was no denying that demons had a fascination with blood, which explained why it was an important ingredient in so many black-magic spells.

Could I use blood to save Matt and me?

I was only a beginner in black magic, and I wanted to keep it that way. My mind struggled for a solution until I realized I needed to be true to myself and use my own magic, however weak, against a powerful demon like Asmodeus.

He shook the car again, flinging us against our seatbelts.

You have defied me, the demon's words thundered in my head. *You will surrender to my will, or I will crush you like a cockroach.*

"Can't you do something?" Matt shouted to me as his truck shook again.

My heart was pounding, and my mind raced. I couldn't think of a spell to save us, and my protection spell wouldn't help us for much longer. Maybe I should just surrender to the demon after all.

Obnoxious shouting stole my attention. It was the driver of the electric truck that had rear-ended the SUV that had previously smashed into the invisible Asmodeus. The man marched to the SUV, waving his arms.

"You freaking idiot!" he screamed at the driver of the SUV,

his face in her open window. "Why did you stop in the middle of the highway?"

"I hit something," replied the SUV's driver, a woman who appeared to have children with her. "I can't see what it was."

"You don't have a clue what you're doing!" The driver shouted, coming up to the SUV's window. "Women shouldn't be allowed to drive. It's gonna cost a fortune to fix my truck, even with insurance. I ought to sue you, you idiot!"

The bully had a shaved head and an earring. He was seething with rage and obviously enjoyed intimidating the poor woman.

He wiped blood from his nose with the back of his hand. Ah, it was *his* blood I had sensed.

I finally knew what to do. Despite my anxiety from being in a truck suspended in the air, I cleared my mind and went into a semi-trance, gathering my internal energies. I enhanced them with the five elemental energies, concentrating on that of earth, affiliated with mineral-rich blood.

Then, I cast a spell that I had learned from Don Mateo, written in his grimoire in a chapter dealing with alchemy. The spell masked the characteristics of my blood, giving it the illusion of being liquid gold and preventing Asmodeus from smelling it.

Here was the key part: I used the same spell on the blood trickling from the nose of the loudmouth on the road beneath me. However, I made his blood mimic the type and characteristics of mine. Increasing its odor, I sent it wafting up to Asmodeus.

The demon appeared confused. The blood that bonded him to me was no longer inside the truck he held aloft. It flowed through the veins and arteries of the human standing on the roadway below.

How could the demon confuse a bald man with me? The demon, only temporarily in the flesh, didn't have a logical brain like you or me. And the magical power of blood drowned out the minimal logic the entity had.

Suddenly, the truck dropped and landed with a jolt on the roadway below, the shock absorbers banging.

"Holy mackerel!" Matt exclaimed.

We were one lane over from the accident, facing the two wrecked cars. An oncoming car rocketed toward us, brakes screeching, and swerved around us onto the shoulder.

I stared through the windshield as a gigantic hand with claw-like nails reached down from above. The bald guy, screaming obscenities into the window of the SUV, was plucked off the roadway and lifted into the sky to face the three heads of Asmodeus. I wondered if the demon was still invisible to him. Probably not.

"Let's go!" I shouted at Matt. "Asmodeus thinks he's bonded to that guy right now, but my spell won't last long."

"You fooled a demon?"

"Believe it or not, yes. I guess being evil doesn't always make you an evil genius."

"What will happen to that jerk he grabbed?"

"When Asmodeus realizes he's been fooled, he'll probably just drop the guy. Unless he eats him."

"Demons eat people?" Matt asked, horrified.

"Occasionally. Not for sustenance, just for punishment. It's what happened to Don Mateo when he summoned a demon by mistake."

"A mistake is putting it lightly."

A few minutes later, when we were too far away to see the towering demon, I added, "He's going to come after me again. I can't rely on illusions to save me. I need help."

"You should talk to Angela."

"I don't think even a mage like her can save me."

"I can't save you," Angela said from behind the front desk of the public library, where she was working the early shift. "I know very little about demonology, and I simply don't have the magic to sever your bond with him. You'll need black magic to do that, unfortunately."

"Yeah," I replied darkly. "My mother could do it, but she won't. There's got to be another way to get him to go away."

"I promise I'll search through all my grimoires and speak with the elder witches I know. If I learn anything, I'll tell you right away."

I thanked her and went home, dejected and scared. Never in all my years had I imagined I'd have a demon problem and how dangerous it could be. Not to mention the inconvenience. I was supposed to be solving the murder of Claire Fusseldink and the collateral deaths from the escaped worm. I also had a day job, as my partner, Luisa, had been reminding me. My work at the botanica had suffered thanks to my distractions.

When I arrived home, the evil energy was palpable.

Great, I thought. Asmodeus isn't letting up.

I turned off my security wards and went inside, using a

simple spell that helped me locate evil entities. Turning on all the lights, I crept carefully through the house. In my bedroom, a green glow leaked from beneath the bed, the spell indicating that benevolent creatures, the cats, were hiding there.

I found no sign of evil until I opened the laundry room door. Red light poured through the crack at the bottom of the door leading to the garage. My stomach dropped. Tony was out there. Was he in danger?

I turned the handle and opened the door slowly. A small amount of orange light from the setting sun seeped through the side window. As my eyes adjusted to the dimness, I looked around and didn't see my iguana witch's familiar, not on the mounted tree branch he used as a perch or on the shelf where he sometimes slept. I flicked on the light switch.

And stifled a scream. Tony clung upside down from a wiring conduit on the unfinished ceiling. His eyes glowed red.

"Tony? Are you okay?"

Because of Ruth's spell, he shouldn't have been able to answer, but he did. "Tony isn't here. I am Asmodeus."

"Leave my lizard alone!"

The temperature in the room dropped suddenly, making my breath turn to frost. Tony projectile-vomited in my direction, then turned his head nearly 360 degrees.

"I'm not impressed by your reenactment of *The Exorcist*," I said, trying to sound brave. "You have no right to be in my house. Leave now!"

"Oh, I have every right to be here," Tony said in a raspy voice that wasn't his. The incongruity of it made me shiver. "You belong to me, and so does your home. I could eat you and your animals right now if I wanted to."

Okay, that reinforced the fact that demons eat people.

"I want to break the bond between us," I said.

"No. You will practice black magic, and we will serve each other. I will give you the power you need to be a powerful sorceress. And you will give me more access to this terrestrial world."

"I'm sorry, but it's just not right for me."

The most horrifying, phlegmy laugh came from Tony's mouth. It sounded almost like Ruth's. "You do not decide what's right for you. Return to me, or I'll eat your cats, then you. The lizard will be last. I don't care for reptile meat. Change your mind quickly, because I will be back for you soon."

Tony dropped to the floor, limp. I picked him up, examined him for injuries, and placed him on the workbench. "Are you hurt?"

He shook his head. Ruth's spell prevented him from telling me anything else.

"Tony, I need to get rid of this demon, but I can't. Ruth won't help me. And Angela doesn't have the magic to release me from my bond. Can you think of anyone who could help me?"

He did several pushups, the lizard version of nodding.

I picked him up and hurried into the kitchen, where the Ouija board still sat on the table. As soon as he was set down, he grabbed the planchette and moved it from letter to letter.

A-G-N-E-S

"Agnes, the vampire?" I asked.

He did his push-up nods and moved the planchette to the upper left of the board where it said, "yes."

"What power would a vampire have against a demon?"

He moved the planchette again, spelling:

O-L-D

I snorted. “Yeah, she’s old, but how does that matter? You’re saying old vampires can defeat demons?”

Tony angrily pushed the planchette to the upper right of the board, over the word “Yes.” How did I know he was angry? Iguanas aren’t shy about hiding their emotions. If you don’t believe me, go to a South Florida park and when you find a mature iguana (which you inevitably will), insult it and see how it reacts.

I said, “I don’t understand how Agnes could help me.”

Tony slid the planchette to the bottom of the board, over the word “Goodbye.” Then he stormed out of the kitchen, tail twitching with frustration.

CHAPTER 13

VAMPIRE VS. DEMON

Sitting on a folding chair, listening to elderly vampires read their cringe-worthy short stories and poems, I briefly questioned why I still ran a creative writing group at Squid Tower every other week. The pay from the homeowners' association was paltry, and I no longer spent most of my working hours at the undead retirement community as a home-health nurse.

The fact was, I felt emotionally attached to the senior vampires who had been turned late in life, their twilight years turning into a twilight that would last for an eternity. There was something cute and endearing about the bewilderment with which so many of them dealt with their vampirism.

Cute and endearing, that is, when they didn't accidentally attack me, like Mrs. Steinhauer had while I was administering blood work. That was what led me to quit working as a nurse, a decision sweetened by a large grant from the Friends of Cryptids Society that set me up full time at the Jellyfish Beach Mystical Mart and Botanica.

Tonight, I was scheduled to meet with Agnes immediately after the writing class. That night's session was less painful than usual. Gladys read her soft-core porn masquerading as romantasy, but it had fewer groan-inducing double-entendres than usual. Walt Whitman had ended his foray into dirty limericks and returned to an inspiring free-verse poem like those he had written when he was alive. The others who had volunteered to read their work offered stories that were filled with clichés but were blessedly short.

When the class was over, I stacked the folding chairs in the community room and headed for the beach, where Agnes had told me she'd be. I walked down the hall past the card room, where a bevy of elderly vampires played canasta and sipped fresh blood from IV bags from the blood-donation bus that arrived nightly like a food truck. In a tiny theater, half a dozen seniors sat in the darkness watching a weepy romance movie on a large TV screen. All I could see of them were silhouettes of the backs of heads and pointy ears.

I went outside into the pool area and crossed the deck. A pool aerobics class was in progress beneath the light of a half-moon. Even preternaturally strong vampires needed to stay in shape if they had been turned with geriatric bodies. I entered a path leading through manicured landscaping that gradually sloped upwards on the rear face of the sand dunes. Atop the dunes was a wooden boardwalk that allowed you to cross over to the beach without damaging the delicate ecosystem of sea oats and sea grape bushes that anchored the dunes in storm tides.

Agnes sat on the bench on the crossover, gazing at the waves rolling in on the deserted beach. It was midnight, so no humans were around. Even if there had been, strict HOA bylaws prohibited residents from feeding on any humans foolish enough to venture onto this stretch of beach at night. Fortunately, there was something instinctual in us, retained since our caveman days, that warned us when predators were nearby.

It didn't stop me from sitting next to one on the bench.

"How was the creative writing class, dear?" Agnes asked.

"It was bearable for once."

"Tell me, what is this issue with a demon you wanted to see me about?"

"Tony, my witch's familiar, believes you have experience with demons. Is that true?" I didn't mention that all he'd communicated was that she was super old.

"Yes, I tangled with a few back in the day. Humans usually put vampires and demons together in the same bucket of evil supernatural entities, but we're entirely different. And vampires are not evil as a whole. We have rare evil individuals, but so do humans. Demons try to manipulate us just as they do your species."

"Really?"

"Demons were a much bigger problem when I was alive. We Visigoths had been Germanic pagans and converted to Christianity by the time I was born. But the world was different back then, at the beginning of the Dark Ages. Demons roamed the earth with impunity, sowing chaos and destruction, goading humans into useless wars and cruelty. My people were forced to repel demons more than once. Krampus, for instance.

But he's a pussycat compared to the others. I personally fought two different demons after I became a vampire."

"Can you help free me from a demon? I used magic recently to trick him into believing another human's blood was mine, but it was just a temporary illusion. I want to free myself from him permanently."

"Which demon? Do you know its name?"

"Asmodeus."

She exhaled sharply. "Goodness gracious. I've met him before. One of the very worst. How did you get bonded to him?"

I explained how Ruth was testing my loyalty and magical prowess and summoned the demon to help me create a powerful doppelgänger spell to break Matt out of jail. "Asmodeus wants me to remain bonded to him and become a black-magic sorceress. I don't want to. When I turned him down, he became ornery."

Agnes laughed. "Oh, he can be ornery, all right."

"Ruth said she's the only one who can break the bond and set me free. And she won't do it unless I remain her student and disciple in black magic. Do you know of another way I can break free?"

"I assume your bond was forged with blood. Correct? That's the most common method."

"Yep."

"As you can imagine, no one knows blood like vampires do."

"Yes, you're connoisseurs of it. How does that help you fight demons?"

"We drink their blood. Just like with any prey, it gives us more power to mesmerize them and make them obey us."

"Demons have blood?"

"When they're in material form, yes. Although I must say some of them have nasty blood." She grimaced. "The last one I defeated had blood that burned my stomach like I was drinking antifreeze."

"Do you believe you could make a demon as powerful as Asmodeus obey you?"

"Demon blood is much stronger than human blood, making my mesmerizing stronger. I only need to control him for a moment. Just long enough for him to break the bond between you two willingly."

"That's amazing." I wasn't sure about Agnes's strategy, but she seemed confident enough.

"Summon him here now," she said. "Let's get this over and done with."

"Maybe we should have additional vampires to back you up."

"Nonsense. I may look small and old, but I'm the most powerful vampire in Squid Tower. Now, get on with it."

Having been the daughter of a Visigoth warrior some 1,500 years ago, Agnes was fearless. But she seemed a little too nonchalant about facing a demon, in my opinion.

"After I summon him, I will cast a protection spell if we need it," I offered.

She nodded impatiently.

I couldn't summon a demon straight from hell, but since I was already bonded with Asmodeus, I figured I could convince him to show up. If I activated the black magic for the original doppelgänger spell Ruth had used him for, I would be on the same frequency as the demon. Judging from his ambush on the highway, and his visit to my garage, he was already very eager to see me.

Lacking a knife, I used a fingernail to tear the scab covering the wound on my palm. When droplets of blood appeared, I cast the beginning of the doppelgänger spell and repeatedly chanted the demon's name.

"Almighty Asmodeus," I intoned, concluding my invocation, "I humbly summon you here to the material world."

Nothing happened. Agnes and I waited while the surf growled on the beach beyond us.

"When Ruth summoned him, she used special incense," I whispered, as if loud talking would scare away a demon. "I don't know what was in it."

"You say he wants to own you," Agnes said, also in a whisper. "He'll come if he senses an opportunity to claim you."

We continued to wait. My summoning attempt had failed. Then, goosebumps broke out on my arms as a cold breeze of dark energy swept over me.

A creaking of wood came from the bottom of the stairs leading to the beach. A higher step groaned more loudly, straining under a tremendous weight. Agnes and I exchanged glances. She quickly crawled under the bench to hide.

Soon, the dark silhouette of three heads appeared, followed by the torso and wings of Asmodeus. The demon climbed until he stood on the boardwalk, towering over me. Yet he was much smaller than he had been when he attacked Matt's truck on the highway. I guessed he chose his size to fit the situation.

"Have you changed your mind?" he asked. His raspy voice wasn't loud, but it penetrated my ears like an awl hammered into my skull. "If not, I shall kill you tonight."

I backed away from him, inching toward the path leading to the condo tower, while I cast my protection spell. First, it would surround me. I would send it to cover Agnes if she got into trouble.

"You're afraid of me?" Asmodeus asked, his face on the human head sneering.

"You were supposed to give me magical powers." My trembling voice betrayed that yes, I was afraid of him. "Why are you acting like I'm your slave?"

"Surely you understood the concept of selling your soul to the Devil? Yes, I will give you almost unlimited power. But at a price." He strutted closer to me on his rooster legs. "I need human agents on Earth to do my bidding and sustain me."

Growls came from behind the demon that sounded like a dog from hell. It was actually a vampire from Unit 805. Agnes leaped into the air and landed on the demon's back, burrowing her face between his human and goat heads, trying to find a vein with her fangs. With her tiny size, she looked like a squirrel attacking a bear.

Asmodeus roared with anger and shook his body, trying to dislodge the geriatric vampire. Agnes held onto the demon's upper back while his heads twisted on their necks, unable to bite her behind them. The demon's hands reached for her while she deftly squirmed away from them.

I transferred my protection spell to her. Because she was pressed so closely against her enemy's back, the spell's bubble was not closing properly. What else could I do to help her? I had to hurry before she lost the struggle to get her fangs into the human neck.

My repertoire of spells was mainly meant for healing and

protection, but I did know how to lob a stink bomb at Asmodeus. Nah, that wouldn't work. Demons loved terrible smells. I had a special affinity for magic powered by the element of air and could shoot microbursts of intense wind. Nah, if I knocked him over, he might trap Agnes beneath his bulk.

What about the element of fire? Improvising, I conjured flames that engulfed Asmodeus's legs. You'd think spitting fire from his mouth and dwelling in the eternal flames of hell would make him immune to fire, but apparently his legs weren't. Sure enough, the rooster feathers that covered them erupted in flames, and he danced about in agony, his snake tail twisting back and forth.

When Asmodeus bent over to slap at the fire, Agnes got her opening. She sank her fangs into the neck of his human head and worked her jaws as she gulped his blood hungrily. He finally removed her from his back with a swat, sending her onto the floorboards of the dune crossover. She bounced slightly when she landed, thanks to the protective bubble that had sealed itself around her.

She stood and made a bloody smile while the demon swayed on unsteady feet, charred by the fire that had gone out.

"Begone, Asmodeus," Agnes commanded in a hypnotic voice. "Break the bond that ties you to Missy and leave this world now. You will obey me because you want to."

He disappeared, literally in a puff of smoke.

"Wow," I said. "Is he really gone?"

Agnes dropped to the floor and convulsed. I rushed over and saw her eyes roll backwards as she trembled in some kind of seizure. It abruptly ended, and she opened her eyes, smiling at me. “No, I’m still here.”

The voice that came from her mouth was Asmodeus’s. The demon had possessed her.

Then, she lunged toward me.

CHAPTER 14

EXPRESS EXORCISM

I immediately transferred my protection spell back to myself with no time to spare. The vampire who was supposed to be my friend lunged at me and hit the bubble with the force of a truck, bouncing off it while sending me flying onto the walking path.

"You lured me into an ambush," she said in Asmodeus's raspy voice. "I will punish you for that."

The cognitive dissonance of Agnes treating me like prey, while speaking in the demon's voice, threw me off balance. And her eyes glowing like burning charcoal didn't help, either. I gathered my energies, preparing to cast my wind spell, and simultaneously added energy to my protection spell. She leaped at me and was blocked again, but I feared I couldn't stop her for much longer. I retreated toward the condo tower.

"Help!" I called, hoping the vampires in the pool would rescue me. Then again, seeing their HOA president trying to feed on me might trigger their own predatory instincts.

I cast my wind spell, clutching the Red Dragon talisman I kept in my pocket to multiply the power of my magic. A focused gust of wind swept across the back lawn, ripping out a piece of shrubbery. It slammed into Agnes and pushed her backward onto the dune crossover.

She shrieked with fury and sprinted toward me. Another, stronger gust hit her and knocked her to the ground, rolling her like a tumbleweed. But this battle was not sustainable. I turned and ran like a panicked child onto the pool deck.

"Help! Agnes is possessed by a demon and wants to kill me!"

Leonard Schwartz, a former home-health patient of mine, looked up at me with annoyance as he soaked up the moonlight on a lounge chair. The participants in the pool aerobics class ignored me completely as they did their exercises. Henrietta rolled past me on her mobility scooter, the only one to notice frenzied Agnes racing across the lawn toward us.

"Henrietta! Please help me! Agnes has been possessed by a demon."

The confusion on Henrietta's face turned to comprehension and finally to concern. Agnes's friend rolled her scooter into Agnes's path at the last moment. Agnes hit it with colossal force, flew into the air, and splashed down into the swimming pool.

At first, the exercisers were annoyed, but when Agnes attacked them, the mob of vampires in seventy- and eighty-year-old bodies surrounded and attempted to subdue her.

"She bit me!" Mrs. Steinhauer screamed.

"Girls, restrain her!" Henrietta shouted. "For her own safety."

"Jeez, I'm just tryin' to relax here," Schwartz complained. He got off the lounge chair and shuffled to the pool. In his skimpy bathing suit beneath his protruding potbelly, he behaved as if his saggy, alabaster-white body was irresistible to the women bathers. He did a cannonball dive into the pool and joined the crowd trying to contain the savage beast Agnes had become. Seized and squeezed by nine vampires, she finally stopped fighting.

"I like the feeling of us together, half-naked like this," Schwartz said to the woman crunched beside him.

"Don't be such a pig," she replied.

I stood on the edge of the pool, looking down at Agnes. "Asmodeus, leave her body. Your fight is with me."

"I rather like being a vampire," the raspy voice said defiantly.

"Agnes will be kept in restraints until we get you to release her. You can't attack me if she's tied down."

"Oh, I'll attack you. Just you wait."

"How are we going to get the demon to leave her?" Henrietta asked me. "I've never encountered a demon before."

"We'll conduct an exorcism."

"That's a real thing?"

"Yes. And I know just the defrocked priest to do it."

Ex-Father Marco Rivera-Hernandez pulled up at my house in his 1965 Ford Mustang. The lanky man in jeans and a surfer shirt unfolded himself from the car and walked to my front door, smiling at me. He had long black hair and a beard that had turned completely white when he became possessed by a demon years ago.

You see, ex-Father Marco had been performing an exorcism, when the rite went sideways and the demon possessed him. Soon afterward, he was defrocked because of frequent unacceptable behavior caused by the demon. The demon was still in him to this day.

"Thanks for coming, Marco."

"It's been a long time, Missy. If I recall, I had tried to help when your garden gnome was possessed?"

"Yes. And here you are to help with another possession. Please come in. Would you like some tea?"

He followed me into the kitchen, where I put the kettle on the stove. "Is your iguana the possessed one? He's speaking to me in American Sign Language, which is not natural for an iguana."

I turned away from the stove and saw Tony in the doorway to the dining room, gesturing to ex-Father Marco with his fore claws.

"No," I replied. "Tony is my witch's familiar and highly intelligent. He can speak English, but he's been silenced by a black-magic spell. I really ought to learn sign language. What's he saying?"

"He's complaining about his food. He wants me to tell you it's not fresh enough."

I sighed with exasperation. "Anyway, the possessed person is a vampire living in Squid Tower. Agnes, the nest mother. Are you okay with exorcising a vampire?"

He grew pale. “I never knew vampires *could* become possessed.”

“Apparently, they can. The demon is Asmodeus.”

“My word. He’s much more powerful than the demon in me—Clarence from Pittsburgh.”

“Will you ever be free of him?”

Ex-Father Marco’s eyes rolled backward. “You bet your butt he won’t,” said a voice that sounded like James Earl Jones.

Marco’s eyes returned to their normal position, and he added in his real voice, “Sorry about that. You know how it is when Clarence takes me over.”

“Do you think Clarence can convince Asmodeus to leave Agnes?”

“I doubt it, but it’s worth a try. Asmodeus is so powerful that the traditional exorcism ritual might not work, so we need all the help we can get. There’s another thing.” He paused and sipped from the cup of tea I had just served him. “I just don’t know if I have the juice for an exorcism anymore. It’s been several years since I was kicked out of the priesthood. I’m afraid Asmodeus won’t respect me.”

“He’s a powerful demon, but he’s not the sharpest pencil in the box. He can be tricked. I did it twice.”

“Demons are the greatest tricksters in the world. If you trick him, he will punish you severely. Before he eats you.”

“Uh-oh.”

My heart ached when I saw Agnes in her bed, snarling and trying to break free from the steel cables that restrained her. The vampires had been considerate enough to put a cushion of blankets between the chains and her flesh, but the ferocity with which she jerked and twisted showed that she felt no pain.

Henrietta, keeping bedside watch, turned her tear-stained face toward us. "This is the priest?"

"*Former* priest and exorcist," Marco said. "I'm Marco Hernandez."

"Henrietta Peters. Thank you for coming. Will you perform the exorcism soon?"

"I'll begin tonight. If the Catholic rites offend you—"

"All that legendary nonsense about vampires abhorring Christian rituals is completely false."

"You mean a crucifix won't bother you?"

"Well, if you *touched* me with one, there might be some burning of flesh."

"Okay, I won't do that with Agnes. There are other methods." He pulled a small glass bottle from his pocket.

Henrietta inched her scooter away from Agnes. "Is that holy water?"

"Holy vodka. If it doesn't drive the demon away, it will make a great martini."

"Let's go wait in the living room so ex-Father Marco can get to work," I said, leading Henrietta from the room. I closed the bedroom door behind us.

"How can you live with yourself knowing that this possession is your fault?" she asked, moving from her scooter into an armchair.

Her question stung. "Agnes insisted on helping me. It was

her idea to lure the demon here in the flesh and drink his blood. No one ever imagined he would possess her. He never possessed me despite having plenty of opportunities."

"I suppose a human host is boring compared to a vampire."

"Get away from me, you hack!" Asmodeus's voice boomed from the bedroom.

I sat on the couch and prayed that Marco would prevail.

Marco prayed aloud in Latin, his voice rising in volume over the bestial groans and growls coming from Agnes. I broke out in a sweat. With my witchy senses, I felt intense power surging from the bedroom: warm, benevolent holiness battling icy-cold, evil magic. Henrietta looked uneasy. The lights in the condo flickered.

A body crashed against the wall. I hoped Marco was okay but dared not enter the room. Glass shattered, probably from a mirror.

"By the power of God, I command you to leave this innocent woman," ex-Father Marco shouted. "By the power of Christ, I command you! By the power of the Holy Spirit, I command you!"

"Is that holy water you're splashing on me?" Asmodeus asked. "It tastes like vodka. Give me some more."

The exorcism was not going well. Marco had told me once that exorcisms often require several sessions, but I worried that might be too dangerous, given the power of Asmodeus and the lethality of vampires should Agnes escape her restraints.

Marco crashed against the wall again. I considered going into the bedroom and calling an end to the session. But then I heard James Earl Jones's voice.

"Asmodeus, baby. How have you been?" It was the demon, Clarence.

"I've been better," the familiar, raspy voice replied.

"Why are you possessing that old crone? You deserve better than that."

"Why are you still possessing a defrocked priest?"

"Give me a break, man," Clarence said with a laugh. "Defrocked priests get to go on dates, have love lives. This guy's a regular Casanova."

"Seems like a dork to me."

"All humans are, when you think about it. Vampires, too. Come on, man, you're a king of demons. With all due respect, you shouldn't be slumming it by possessing mortal creatures. Or undead ones."

"I should have possessed the witch who defied me," Asmodeus said.

"What's the point of that? Isn't it better to make her obey your orders than to operate her body like a puppeteer? You command legions of demons. You can't do that when you're stuck in someone's body."

"I see your point."

"I'm just giving you friendly advice, demon to demon . . . hello? Are you in there?"

"Why am I tied up?" Agnes asked. "Someone, help me!"

I rushed into the bedroom. Agnes looked at me from the bed, her eyes sharp and her expression normal. "Missy, what happened to me?"

"After you attacked the demon, he got revenge by possessing you."

"He was supposed to be mesmerized."

"Your mesmerization powers weren't strong enough for him."

Agnes shook her head in frustration. "I only needed to control him for a moment." She finally noticed ex-Father Marco, who was lying on the floor. "Who is that human?"

"Your savior." I explained the exorcism and Clarence's intervention.

"I had the strangest dream. He was in it. He's kind of cute, isn't he?"

Henrietta entered the room on her mobility scooter. "What in the world were you thinking, Agnes? Attacking a demon? Even a powerful vampire like you can't beat a demon."

Neither can a witch like me, and that's a problem, I thought. *Because Asmodeus will come after me again.*

CHAPTER 15
AFFAIRS OF THE HEART

I held my phone and stared at the photo of Jude Levings and Claire Fusseldink. He wore a suit, and she looked splendid in a cocktail dress. They stood side by side, smiling at the camera, their bodies touching. He appeared to have a hand on her back. It was the typical kind of photo taken at galas and fundraising events. With their body language suggesting familiarity and intimacy, you would have thought they were a married couple.

"That picture is from the Cryptozoology Association holiday party," Matt said as he drove his truck.

"Must have been the hottest ticket in town."

"Don't be sarcastic. You're part of that weird world, remember? Anyway, the party took place after Levings and his staff returned from Mongolia, and Milo was believed to be missing. I found the membership list and asked around for rumors about an affair. There's always gossip in organizations like these. Of course, I got a lot of verbal abuse for my questions."

"No wonder. But you're a hard-nosed reporter. You can handle it."

"One person, a professional rival of Levings, said she believed some hanky-panky was going on. It wasn't enough to prove anything, but enough to convince me we're on the right track."

"I think making this trip to question Zora again is a waste of time. She's turned hostile toward us."

"You'll use your truth spell on her."

"I can try," I said. "But I'm having my doubts about the spell. Milo didn't act like I'd expected when I used it on him. I spoke to Angela, and she told me spells like this can be overcome by super-intelligent people. You could say that Milo is a genius, though a kooky one."

"You mean he was lying to us? Like, he really *did* bring a worm back from Mongolia and put it in the house to kill his wife?"

"I don't know. Maybe. I'm just saying we can't rely on my truth spell to work a hundred percent of the time."

"I guess it's like a polygraph. The test can give you a good idea if someone is lying, but it's not reliable enough to use in court."

"I love magic. I really do," I said with passion. "It can help us solve crimes, but it can't put criminals behind bars. What worries me is what the Cryptids Society would do to Claire's murderer before he or she is turned over to the police. I don't want my magic to result in someone being mistreated."

A sense of dread filled me as my imagination conjured up images of Milo or Levings thrown into a jail cell with strange monsters at the Cryptid Sanctuary.

"Your magic can point us in the right direction for our investigations," Matt reminded me. "Let's take one step at a time and find out if Levings had a motive to kill Claire Fusseldink. Don't worry about the Society right now."

MATT HAD FOUND Zora's address, and we drove to her apartment complex, not far from the university. She emerged twenty minutes before noon and drove a small, decrepit car to the campus. We didn't follow her inside the building she entered because she was probably teaching an undergraduate class or meeting with someone. We waited in Matt's truck parked near her car.

Matt took a deep breath. "So. . ."

I studied his furrowed brow, his folded arms. "Yes?"

"Things haven't been the same between us. You've been kind of distant."

"I'm being stalked by a demon. My witch's familiar has been silenced by black magic. There's at least one death worm slithering around killing people. And we're investigating a murder and a possible extramarital affair, with all the weight on our shoulders to solve it. Are you truly surprised that I have a lot on my mind?"

"Not when you put it that way. I just want to make sure everything's okay with us."

"Everything's peachy."

"You sound sarcastic."

"Matt, now is not the time to talk about our relationship.

We're best friends and we're sometimes intimate. Let's enjoy what we have and not overanalyze it."

"I'm neurotic. It's in my nature to overanalyze. I also need to feel loved."

I sighed, which probably didn't help matters. "I love you."

"I love you, too. Perhaps too much."

"Don't say 'too much.'"

"We've discussed this before. I want to settle down and have a family. You're focused on otherworldly things."

"Yes, we have discussed this. I'm at the age where it would be difficult to have kids. And I don't want to bring children into a world where I might get killed by a demon or any variety of monsters."

"A family can be just the two of us." He was moping. "I know I can't change your mind. I can't get you to focus on the boring life of a human guy when you're obsessed with magic and monsters. I'm just venting, okay?"

"I'm not obsessed," I said a bit too forcefully. "Someday, soon, I'll slow down and learn to appreciate the simpler things in life. The people I care about most." I kissed his cheek. "Someday, soon, I won't spend so much time on magic. Once I've reached my true potential and strongest powers."

"Ah, I'm beginning to understand what's come over you." He stared into my eyes as if he could diagnose my emotional turmoil. "You're trying to push yourself to the next level."

"That's a good way of putting it," I said. But what I thought was, *that's better than saying I'm drunk on power, because I'm afraid I am.*

"She's coming out now."

Zora exited the building, wearing a preoccupied frown, and drove off. We followed. She ended up at a familiar place: the university's bookstore cafe. We waited, giving her time to get settled, then went inside. She sat at a small table with a cup of coffee and a thick, printed manuscript she appeared to be editing with a pencil.

"Is that a book you wrote?" I asked.

She looked up and wasn't happy to see us.

"No. It's by Dr. Levings. Why are you guys here?"

"Pure happenstance," Matt lied. "But if you don't mind, we have just a few questions to ask you, and then we'll leave you alone."

"I'm very busy."

"We'll be quick," I said, sitting across from her, uninvited. I reached into my pocket for the packet of powder for my truth spell, gathered my energies, and began silently to recite the incantation.

Matt stood behind me because there wasn't a third chair. "I saw the words 'death worms' on the page," he said. "Is that what the book is about?"

"Yes. Now, if you don't mind—"

"That's the same topic as the book Milo Fusseldink is writing. When we spoke with Dr. Levings, he didn't mention he was writing about it, too."

"He doesn't believe you should talk about works-in-progress, except with your collaborators and publisher. Is this really what you want to talk to me about?"

Just as I completed the spell's incantation, I reached beneath the table and sprinkled the powder on Zora's feet.

"To be honest, no," Matt replied. He looked at me to see if he needed to continue stalling for time.

Zora's eyes had the telltale glassy look with dilated pupils. Her face became more animated. The spell had taken effect. I nodded to Matt. It was time for me, the weaver of the spell, to take over.

I leaned over and made my face level with hers. "Was Dr. Levings having an affair with Claire Fusseldink?"

When asked uncomfortable questions, people under the truth spell often struggle with their magically induced urge to tell the truth and their need to avoid doing so. Not Zora. She eagerly answered, as if her secret had built up so much steam it was about to burst out of her. "Yes, he was having an affair with that horrible woman."

"Was the affair still going on when she died?"

"No."

"Who broke up with whom?"

"I don't know," she said, her eyes wide open and her tongue licking her lips. "Dr. Levings kept calling her afterwards."

"How do you know that?"

"I walked into his office several times while he was doing it."

"Did it seem like he was on a friendly call?" I asked.

"No. He acted very frustrated. One time, he was shouting when I walked into his office."

"When did the affair end?"

"I don't know. At some point before we left for Mongolia."

"Did he visit Claire's house while Milo was missing?"

"No. He did before the expedition. Remember, they had separated before we returned."

I paused briefly while I struggled to compose my next question. “You sound hostile toward Claire. Why?”

Zora underwent the struggle to censor herself that I had described earlier. “Claire was horrid.”

“Why? What do you mean?”

“She was a rich snob. I don’t know why she married Dr. Fusseldink, but she had little respect for academia. She was passionate about organizing fundraisers for the university but didn’t seem to care for our mission. She should have married a rich Wall Street guy, not a passionate researcher like Milo. And she should never have toyed with a genius like Dr. Levings. I’m sure he didn’t know how to deal with mercenary women like her.”

I paused again. “Were you jealous of her?”

“Why would I be jealous? Because of her wealth? No, I hated her because of her snobbery about academia. Because she thought we’re silly and useless, whereas she was the one who was useless without her inheritance.”

The spell appeared to be wearing off, so I tried a Hail Mary pass. “Are you attracted to Dr. Levings?”

Her face turned red. “He’s like a father to me, as well as a mentor. I am grateful and loyal to him, and that’s all that matters.”

“One last question. Is there any possibility that Dr. Levings captured a death worm but kept it secret from you and the others on the expedition?”

“Why would he do that? We all uprooted our lives to spend very difficult weeks in the Gobi Desert. If he had found a worm, he would have shared it with us to reward us for our sacrifices. And imagine all the fame he would have gotten in the cryptozoological world. Hiding the worm makes no sense at all."

Yeah, I thought. *It made no sense unless he planned to use the worm as a murder weapon. For Claire, not Milo.*

The glazed look was gone from Zora's eyes, meaning the spell had worn off. She looked at us with surprise, as if she hadn't noticed we'd been here.

"My, what got into me? I was talking and talking like a hyperactive child. I don't even remember what I was saying."

"No worries," I said. "We enjoyed it. You have a very interesting career."

"It seems like I was just talking about gossipy things."

"Anything about cryptozoology is fascinating to me."

Matt made a sharp intake of breath as he stared, riveted, at his phone. "Another one."

"Another what?" Zora asked.

"Fatality on the beach. The same symptoms of poisoning as Claire Fusseldink and the jogger. But not of electrocution, like the golfer."

I stared at Zora's face, searching for signs of guilt showing she knew how the worm got to America. There were none.

"My God," she murmured. "There *is* a worm in Jellyfish Beach. Part of me hoped it was only hype."

"Why would you hope that?" I asked.

"The Mongolian Death Worm has been a mysterious, alluring legend for cryptozoologists for more than a century. It's almost like a religious figure. We've wanted so badly to find one, but at the same time, I didn't want to find one. Because surely, in the flesh, the actual worm would disappoint compared to the legend. And once a specimen was acquired, what would be the point of my career?"

"You could focus on another cryptid," I suggested.

Zora seemed unconvinced.

"Let's go," Matt said to me. "We have a long drive, and I want to get there before they cart the body away."

CHAPTER 16

WORM HUNTING

That night, long after the crime scene had been worked over, we returned to the beach. The moon was half full, bathing the sand in a silver light. At this late hour, and on this stretch of beach beside the golf course, there wasn't a single person around. But was there a worm? Or worms?

"Do you really think there might be more than one?" Matt whispered.

"Dr. Hooey, the ickologist, told us the death worm could reproduce on its own, so it's a good possibility there are others." I shivered at the thought, peering intently at the silver sand, looking for signs of something burrowing beneath the surface.

A torn-open plastic pouch caught my eye. It had probably been dropped accidentally by the crime-scene investigators when we were watching them, forced to remain at a distance by Officer Bird. I put the trash in my pocket so it wouldn't end up in the ocean, harming a bird or sea turtle.

What was unusual about this most recent death was the state of the body. Officer Bird had told us that the victim exhibited signs of having been fed upon. She theorized that crabs had done it, or even coyotes. But Matt and I knew it had been one or more worms.

At the crime scene, there had been no signs of worms. That's why we had returned at night, hoping to spot worm activity in the darkness when they were more active.

We had no idea how to catch a worm if we found one. Or more. We both had our phones ready to take pictures if we saw anything. Matt carried a heavy canvas duffel bag for transporting any specimens we happened to catch. I had an extension grabber with trigger-activated jaws, the tool people used to pick up litter from the ground or grab an item from a tall shelf. I wasn't confident it could securely grasp an angry death worm.

We also wore plastic face shields like orthopedic surgeons use. They would protect our faces from sprays of venom, at least if they were frontal attacks. The shields wouldn't cover streams from the side or rear.

Near where I had picked up the plastic, something caught my eye. A hole in the ground with excavated sand piled around the opening. Ghost crabs live on the beach and dig burrows into the sand, but the holes weren't as large as this one.

"Matt, look at this." I pointed to the opening. "Did a crab do it?"

Matt regularly spent a lot of time on the beach surf fishing. He knew the coastal environment well. "Nope. Not a crab." He crouched beside the hole. “Looks like something pushed itself out of the hole instead of digging in from the outside.”

A blur of movement. A flash of pink and red. Matt screamed as the long, sausage-shaped thing shot out of the hole like a missile from a silo.

Without thinking, I dove at Matt, tackling him and rolling with him in the sand away from the death worm’s spray of toxin. A drop of liquid hit the back of my neck and burned intensely. We scrambled to our feet and ran away from the worm. Only when we were several strides away did I dare to look behind me.

The worm wasn’t chasing us. It had returned to its hole, but half its length remained protruding from the sand. Its body looked like an intestine or an unusually large pork sausage. It watched us, though I didn’t see any eyes, only a horrific round mouth at the end of its tubular body—a yawning red cavity ringed with shark-like triangular teeth. It was waiting for its prey to return to it.

That’s when the opioid-like effects kicked in. The skin on the back of my neck still burned as if from acid, but my heart rate picked up, and a euphoria spread through me.

“I think I’m high,” I said in a quiet voice. “And I want more of this feeling.”

“Yeah, and if you were a small-brained dessert mammal, you would wander back to the worm that gave you the good feeling. And it would try again to kill you. But you know better.”

“Now I understand how drug addicts feel. I’m smart enough to know not to return to the worm, but I sure want to. We have to catch the darn worm.”

"With that flimsy grabber-thing?"

"And with magic. Assuming my spells will work on this creature. Give me a few minutes."

The most obvious magic to try was my trusty sleep spell. I cast it fairly quickly, but it had no effect on the worm. Its head continued to move back and forth as if it were sampling scents in the air, like other reptiles do with their tongues.

"I guess my sleep spell only works on mammals," I said. "Let me try my immobility spell."

I gathered my internal energies, as well as the elemental ones of water and earth from the powerful surf and the tons of sand around me. I soundlessly chanted the incantation. Just as I was sending the magic to the worm, it snapped its head toward me suddenly, sensing danger. It disappeared into the hole.

"Damn," Matt said. "What happened?"

"It must have felt my magic somehow. I guess you can't survive as an undiscovered creature without hypersensitive instincts for fleeing danger."

"Do you think the spell affected it after it went down into its burrow?"

"Maybe. We'd have to dig it out if that's the case. Do you have a shovel?"

"In my truck. Though I'm not happy about the prospect of digging to find that bugger. I'll get the shovel. Wait, what was that?"

"What?"

"That sound."

I strained to hear anything above the crashing surf, but then it came to me: a scratching, sifting sound, like things disturbing the sand near the dunes. Living things. I pulled a high-intensity flashlight from my pocket that I hadn't used tonight, not wanting to scare the death worm. Now, I wanted to scare the crap out of any death worm coming towards us.

And there were at least a dozen. No exaggeration. My flashlight beam swept across the creatures moving towards us, each about the length of my arms and the diameter of my legs. How had a single worm birthed all these critters? And how had they grown so big so quickly?

The death worms slithered in a sidewinding motion like snakes, but their middle sections often undulated from the ground like inchworms. I shuddered at the freakish sight of them.

A dry rustling came from behind me. The original worm had emerged from its burrow again and moved aggressively toward us. If my immobility spell had worked on it, the magic had clearly worn off.

"I think we should get out of here," Matt said.

"We can't leave without capturing at least one of them. There are so many right out in the open." I wasn't being brave, just practical.

"I think the narcotic in the venom is warping your brain."

"Hang on for a moment. Use your flashlight to keep the one behind us at bay."

The worms approaching us from the other side weren't together in a group. They had emerged from the sand in different spots along the beach. The closest one was only a few yards away, its mouth with the jagged teeth opening and closing rhythmically. This worm was hungry.

Before I cast my spell, I wondered why here on the beach,

where there was plenty of prey—unlike in the desert—the worms would attack humans. My theory was that while there were plenty of birds, they were probably uncatchable. Crabs and mollusks were too difficult for the worms to eat. There was an abundance of seaweed washed ashore, but the worms were clearly carnivores.

The ocean lapping upon the beach teemed with fish. However, the worms apparently avoided the sea.

I cast my immobility spell as I retreated from the closest worm creeping toward me. As I'd feared, the spell didn't work. The worm kept wriggling forward. But I had a backup plan and conjured a different spell.

Matt's flashlight beam moved from worm to worm. The bright light stunned them momentarily before they continued moving again. This slowed down their advance, but they had become dangerously close, driving us toward the dunes behind us. We backed toward a gap between dunes, ready to flee to Matt's truck.

I gathered my energies and grasped the Red Dragon talisman in my pocket for extra power. And I cast a spell that I had first learned when my home's air conditioning went on the fritz. This time, however, I used it on an industrial scale.

It was a cold spell. From my outstretched arms blew a blast of Arctic air, focused and powerful as if from a leaf blower. It struck the nearest worm with infallible aim.

The worms were used to the brutal heat of the desert, but even the cold desert nights couldn't prepare them for the icy subzero air. The nearest worm immediately curled into a ball like a centipede.

"Matt! Open your duffel bag for an incoming worm!"

I raced toward the cold-stunned worm and grasped it with my grabber tool. The creature was heavier than I had expected. Matt had come up behind me, and I swung around, dropping the specimen into the bag. He hurriedly zipped it shut.

"Let's go!" I shouted.

We ran uphill on a narrow path between two dunes. Just as we saw the road ahead, a dark shape slithered across the sand, blocking our way.

"Another freaking worm?" Matt wailed.

Without thinking, I swung the grabber tool like a golf club and knocked the worm to the side, into the saucer-like leaves of sea grape bushes. Liquid splashed upon my plastic face shield. A few drops hit my ear and burned fiercely.

A few seconds later, ecstasy filled me. "I want more," I said.

Matt yanked my arm and dragged me away from the dunes and onto the dirt shoulder of the road. He pulled me toward his truck, parked beneath a streetlamp.

I fought the call of the euphoric feelings. "I'm okay. You can let go of me."

Matt put the duffel bag in the truck bed. The bag bulged and thrashed as the worm recovered from my spell. Matt looked at me and frowned. "You have some nasty burns on your ear and the back of your neck."

"I'll be fine. Let's get this worm off our hands."

Right after we got into the cab, a white van pulled up in front of the truck. Mrs. Lupis and Mr. Lopez got out and approached the passenger side of the cab.

I lowered the window. "How did you guys know we were here?"

They smiled, but didn't answer, just as I had expected.

"Congratulations on capturing a worm," Mrs. Lupis said. "Come with us while we take it to the sanctuary."

A goblin in a white jumpsuit uniform bearing the logo of the Cryptid Society got out of the van's driver seat. He retrieved the duffel bag from the truck and placed it in the rear of the van without a word of greeting.

"I'm afraid your paramour can't come," said Mr. Lopez with a wink. "He's not a member of the Society."

"Paramour?" Matt asked.

"Ignore him," I said. "Thanks for your help. I'll be in touch when I'm back in the real world."

While the Cryptid Sanctuary existed in a parallel universe of sorts, it was also a place of unreality, as I would soon experience.

CHAPTER 17

RAPID REPRODUCTION

Dr. Hooey was giddy with excitement while he examined the death worm in his lab. He had injected it with a tranquilizer to reduce our risk of death, but the four of us wore face shields just in case. As he rolled the worm about on the stainless-steel table, traces of venom oozed from its hideous open mouth. The worm's tail was covered with a rubber sock to prevent electrical shock, even though the creature was unconscious.

"Wonderful specimen," he said. "Young, too. It must be a parthenogenetic offspring of the original worm. You say you saw others?"

"Yes," I replied. "There were around a dozen worms on the beach, maybe more."

Dr. Hooey smiled in wonder. "Such incredible creatures."

"Incredibly scary creatures. We need to get rid of them in Jellyfish Beach."

The scientist lost his smile. "It's true that they don't belong here. Florida is beset by invasive species, both conventional and cryptids. Invasive species, like Burmese pythons, are a disaster for our environment and wipe out our native populations. I'm a powerful advocate for removing invasive species. Nevertheless, we are so fortunate to have this incredibly unique one to study."

Mr. Lopez cleared his throat. "If the worms can reproduce so fast, why have none been found in the Gobi Desert?"

"One *was* found," Mrs. Lupis said. "The cause of the mess we're in."

"True, true."

"The desert environment is so extreme," Dr. Hooey said, "the worms don't have enough food to sustain a large population. In fact, the species adapted to survive long periods without eating. With all the humans on the beach here in Florida, it's like an all-you-can-eat buffet for them."

"You're saying they're reproducing so quickly because they have plenty of food?" Mr. Lopez asked.

"Precisely. Also, they're more likely to come to the surface here in Florida. The geological aspects of their natural habitat allow for much deeper burrows than they can dig here. The softer sand on the beach will collapse. Therefore, they can hide more easily in Mongolia and hibernate for longer periods. In the desert, they come to the surface only to feed and drink rainwater. Another reason they've avoided discovery is that there are very few humans about in the desert to spot them. Personally, I believe they have a cunning instinct to avoid us."

"Not anymore," Mr. Lopez muttered.

"They are incredible, aren't they?" asked Mrs. Lupis.

"They ate their last victim's face," I said.

"This sanctuary is full of creatures that eat humans," said Mr. Lopez. "It's in their nature. That doesn't make them bad. Are tigers and grizzlies bad?"

I ignored him and turned back to Dr. Hooey. "If having so many people visiting the beach leads to the worms reproducing quickly, should we close the beaches?"

"Possibly," he replied. "The worms are only following a law of nature. Ample resources encourage larger populations."

"Do the worms feed on fish?"

"Only the fish that are washed up onto the beach. My research makes me believe that the worms can't tolerate saltwater."

"How would you know that without a specimen to examine?"

"By extrapolating data from various reptilians and other species similar to the death worm."

"You are saying the worm *is* a reptile?" Mrs. Lupis asked.

"Partly." The scientist gave a devilish smile. "I suspect it is a hybrid of reptile and worm. The only such creature in the world. Another reason I am so fascinated by it."

"Your job is to study it," Mr. Lopez said. "Unfortunately, our job is to manage cryptid populations, meaning removing them from Jellyfish Beach before they spread throughout the state. Florida's economy would suffer if too many tourists are killed by death worms."

"No kidding," I murmured.

Mr. Lopez pressed on. "Dr. Hooey, do you have any suggestions for how we can eliminate the worms?"

"First, you must work quickly because of their speed of reproduction."

"No kidding," I repeated.

"To lure them out of their burrows so they may be caught more easily, you might try a technique that it appears the expeditions never employed," Hooey continued. "Music."

"*What?*" Mrs. Lupis and Mr. Lopez exclaimed simultaneously.

"Music from a pungi, a flute-like reed instrument made from a gourd. It's used in India to charm snakes because of the high-pitched notes and vibrations it produces."

"How do you know this will work?" Mr. Lopez asked.

"I'm not saying it *will* work. It *might* work. In theory."

I said, "I saw Milo Fusseldink playing an instrument that must have been a pungi. Where can we buy one?"

"Online, of course," Mrs. Lupis and Mr. Lopez said simultaneously.

"Sorry, there are actually things you can't buy online," said Dr. Hooey. "I own a pungi that was handmade in a remote village in India. I will ship it to you, Ms. Mindle."

"Do you guys know how to play a pungi?" I asked my handlers.

"No," Mr. Lopez said. "But you will. After you watch several hours of instructional videos online."

"I'm not very musical. I always sing off-key."

"The worms will not care," Dr. Hooey said. "The important thing is to experiment until you find the notes at the right pitch and can produce the right vibrations. My theory is that the worms will mistake the sound and vibrations for thunderstorms. If I'm correct, the worms will rush from their burrows, expecting to drink the rare rain—their only source of water in the Gobi."

"And then what?"

"You will capture them," Mrs. Lupis said. "And we will dispose of them."

"There are already too many worms for me to capture. And they'll produce more offspring in the meantime. I need help. We need dozens of pungi players and worm hunters."

"First things first," said Mr. Lopez. "Catch as many as you can, and we'll find additional personnel. Thank you for the one captured worm, and good luck for more to come. See you soon."

"Where are you guys going?"

"We can't divulge that information."

"Who's going to drive me home?"

"Frankie. The goblin who drove the van. After he delivers us, he'll return to get you."

My handlers waved goodbye and left the lab. I was left alone with Dr. Hooey, feeling awkward. I didn't know how to make small talk with a scientist, especially one from a different, unidentified species.

"Um, where are you from?" I asked.

"Jellyfish Beach."

"I mean, where did you come from?"

He stopped measuring the worm with calipers and gave me an icy stare. "You ask me that because I speak with an accent? I am an American from Jellyfish Beach. You should realize that such a question is insulting to people who look or speak differently from you."

I felt my face turn red, but I pushed on. "Sorry. I'm only asking because it's been made clear to me that you, Mrs. Lupis, and Mr. Lopez aren't human. In fact, they once lived at the

Sanctuary. I don't even know if they're aliens from another planet. I'm only asking because I joined the Society with a mission to study cryptids, even those in human form."

"You're implying this is not my natural form?"

"Um, no." *How could I get myself out of this mess?* "I apologize for being rude."

Dr. Hooey gave a slight smile. "I understand your curiosity. I will tell you that all three of us are from the Land of Faerie, which is not of this world."

"Ah, so you guys are Fae?"

He shook his head. "Other peoples besides Fae live in the Land of Faerie. That's all I can say for now without the permission of Mrs. Lupis and Mr. Lopez."

I nodded and fidgeted while he continued his work. "Where can I find Frankie to get my ride home?"

"He will come for you."

Still feeling awkward, I couldn't keep my mouth shut. But I tried to keep my questions more pertinent.

"So, where did you go to school to become a cryptozoologist?"

He scanned the unconscious worm with an infrared device I didn't recognize. "I earned my PhD from Swampland University."

"Ah, did you study under Dr. Levings?"

"I took some of his undergraduate classes. Human cryptozoologists see the world in a much narrower way than the rest of us, so I quickly moved on from his tutelage."

"What do you mean by 'narrower'?"

"For them, cryptids are animals, like Sasquatch or the Loch Ness Monster, that are not much different from other creatures except in their exotic nature and elusiveness. As you know, we here at the Friends of Cryptids Society of the Americas are much broader in our views. We include supernatural creatures, such as shifters, in our scope of study, as well as creatures of folklore, such as gnomes and dragons. The basilisk in the other room is a prime example of that."

"I see. Why doesn't someone like Dr. Levings study dragons?" I asked. "Because he mistakenly believes they're extinct?"

"Because Dr. Levings and others like him don't believe in dragons at all. They want so badly to be accepted in the world of respectable human scientists. But they never will. They'll always be branded as pseudoscientists. We at the Cryptic Society are above all that. We study every kind of monster, and I use the term with no moral judgement. It's simply a handy way to label all the species and entities feared by humans. And we do study all of them—even the occasional demon and ghost."

Demon? I thought. *Why haven't I even considered asking for help with Asmodeus from the Society?*

Dr. Hooey continued. "You asked about Mrs. Lupis, Mr. Lopez, and me. We are among those that Dr. Levings and Dr. Fusseldink have no interest in or conception of. They don't know or care that we exist. They're too busy striving for fame and respect from a mainstream scientific community that doesn't take them seriously."

"Do you believe one of them brought the first death worm home and used it to kill Mrs. Fusseldink?"

"It certainly looks like that was the case, doesn't it? Not surprising behavior, really, for embittered men like them. I'll tell you one thing: neither of them deserved to have successfully captured a Mongolian Death Worm."

I'D NEVER BEEN able to get a cellphone signal in the sanctuary, probably because the place wasn't technically on Earth. But as soon as Frankie drove me across the creek and back onto the road to the real-world national wildlife refuge, I noticed I had plenty of bars. As well as a voicemail from Matt.

"Call me as soon as you can. I've got some juicy info about Milo."

I called him immediately. "Whatcha got?"

"Remember when we spoke to the Fusseldinks' neighbor, and she mentioned the police had come to the house when Milo was still living there?"

"Yeah. She thought it was a burglary or something. That's what Claire told her."

"Well, it wasn't," Matt said. "One of my sources, Officer Bird, let it slip that she'd been sent to the house twice for domestic disturbances reported by Claire. Allegedly, Milo had been abusive. Both times, Claire refused to press charges."

"If Milo had a history of violence against her, that could point to him wanting to kill her."

"Right. It's not enough proof in itself, but I think we should focus on Milo again. Despite what he said under the truth spell."

"I guess, then, it's true that highly intelligent people can resist the spell. I need to learn a new one. Did Officer Bird tell you if Milo is still a suspect in his wife's murder?"

"No. She's not in the loop. We would need to ask Shortle. And there's no guarantee she'd tell us."

"I guess it doesn't matter what Shortle thinks. We have to find the killer on our own." I noticed Frankie looking at me in the rearview mirror with his yellow eyes surrounded by hairy, leathery skin. I'd best be careful what I said in his presence. Just because I worked with the Society didn't mean I could fully trust them. "We should find someone who was close to Claire and talk to them about this matter. I'll call you when I get home," I told Matt before disconnecting.

I searched the internet and social media with my phone and quickly found the person we needed to interview. If she agreed to speak with us.

CHAPTER 18
A WORM OF A MAN

After my Society handlers first referred my magical services to Claire Fusseldink, I had spoken with her by phone a couple of times to arrange the spell session in which I would try to locate Milo. Boy, that sure didn't turn out well. Anyway, when Claire and I were trading phone calls, I followed her on social media to learn more about her.

Perusing her feed again was very helpful. Her most active follower was obviously a close friend, and internet searches produced the friend's contact information. Her name was Marcia Clementi, and she lived in Jellyfish Beach. Knowing she was unlikely to consent to meet with strangers, I went heavy on our concern for Claire.

The police are making no progress in solving Claire's murder, I emailed her. *My coworker and I are investigative reporters, and we are trying to bring her justice. Would you be willing to give us a brief meeting?*

It worked. The next day, Matt and I showed up at the high-end law firm downtown where Marcia was a partner. It was in a well-preserved brick building from the 1920s right on the Intracoastal Waterway, with a seafood restaurant on the ground level. We took an elevator to the third floor and were shown into a conference room with a stunning view of the water and the drawbridge. We sipped mineral water until Marcia strode briskly into the room.

She was petite and olive-skinned, with short, curly black hair. Her dress looked like it cost more than my entire wardrobe. Matt and I stood to shake her hand.

Marcia skipped the small talk. "How can you help solve Claire's murder? You're not detectives."

"We have the time and determination to find the truth," Matt said sincerely. "The police do not."

"The official story is that Claire was sprayed in the face with a powerful toxin," Marcia said. "But I've seen rumors on social media that some lethal creature was involved, a snake or something, and that it has killed other people. Is that just another social-media conspiracy theory?"

"In this case, it's true," I replied, having decided to be transparent about the cryptid. "The creature is called the Mongolian Death Worm. And Claire's husband, Milo, devoted years of his life to finding one. We believe he succeeded and brought it home."

Marcia gasped. "I knew that man was no good."

"Milo was believed to be missing in Mongolia, but he was actually in Jellyfish Beach when Claire was killed. He claims to have an alibi, but we don't think it exonerates him. We wanted to ask you about what motives he might have to kill her, and if you believe he was capable of it."

"You wouldn't think a sorry excuse for a man like that would be capable of murder," she said, wiping away a tear. "But yes, I think he was."

"We were told the marriage was under strain," I said.

"Yes. I've known Claire since law school and went to her wedding. When Claire married Milo, he was beginning a career in bioengineering. Suddenly, he turned into a weird conspiracy theorist and took up researching cryptids, if that's what they're called. Stupid legends like Bigfoot. He knew he had Claire's money to fall back on, so he turned his hobby into a pretend career."

"That caused a strain?"

"Among other things," Marcia replied. "They simply weren't compatible. He went on long expeditions to remote places, leaving her behind. He had a bunch of fans—other weirdos like him—which apparently gave him the emotional satisfaction he should have gotten from his wife."

"I know this is a delicate topic," I said, "but did he ever abuse her?"

"Yes. Claire began seeing someone. Why she chose another fake scientist, I don't know. She could have found a much better man."

"Would this person be Dr. Jude Levings, by any chance?" Matt asked.

Marcia looked at him sharply. "Yes. And when Milo found out about the affair, that was when he became abusive. Claire assured me he never harmed her physically, only emotionally. But he constantly threatened to hurt or kill her. She called the police a few times but never pressed charges. Milo eventually moved out of the house, and she broke off the affair with Dr.

Levings. Milo didn't move back in, and then he went off to Mongolia. I was so relieved that she was safe at last. I was terribly wrong."

"Do you believe Milo put the death worm in her bedroom to kill her?"

"It's the cowardly kind of thing he would do. And I can think of no one else who would do it. How ironic: a worm of a man killing his wife with a worm."

"Have the police spoken with you?" Matt asked.

"No, they haven't. I'm grateful that you guys reached out. What can you do to get justice for Claire?"

"We'll destroy Milo's alibi for the night of the murder. And we'll hand the police a neatly wrapped package of evidence against him with a bow on top."

I thought Matt was being overly optimistic, but kept my mouth shut. Instead, I asked, "Is there anything else you'd like to add?"

Marcia's eyes looked up to the left as she thought about it. "I have a question. Is it really true that this death worm is still on the loose?"

"Let's just say you should avoid going to the beach at night."

Thanks to HIPAA privacy regulations, your medical data must remain private unless you authorize it to be shared. Milo must have assumed we wouldn't have a legal way to confirm that he had been in the hospital when Claire was killed.

Yet Milo didn't know that I had once been a nurse. I worked in the intensive care unit, where the stress and emotional toll drove me to take a job as a home health nurse with a company that specialized in supernatural creatures who couldn't use regular doctors. That's how I became a fixture among the vampires at Squid Tower.

Although I had worked in the ICU, Jellyfish Beach Memorial was small enough that I had friends in many other departments. Including the cardiovascular unit. I made a phone call to a nurse friend who owed me a favor, HIPAA be damned.

When my friend checked patient records, she saw no evidence that Milo had been in the cardiovascular unit, nor in the hospital at all, except for some diagnostic testing three years ago. His alibi was demolished.

"I think we should have a little chat with Milo," I said to Matt as we sat in his truck outside the law offices. "We can't depend on my truth spell, but maybe he'll admit something."

"The police won't trust our evidence."

"Doesn't matter. I need to be confident enough in Milo's guilt to refer him to the Cryptid Society's justice department. They can handle the rest."

"It's not as if your job will be done. There are still a bunch of death worms crawling around out there."

I sighed. "Yeah, that's a major problem that's only getting worse. But venomous death worms are much more straightforward foes than devious human murderers."

Matt put the truck into gear. "Let's go talk to the devious murderer."

We drove down to Port Inferno only to find that Milo wasn't home. His car was parked at the storage facility, though, so we grabbed sandwiches and waited nearby for him to leave, then followed him home. We confronted him just as he was unlocking his apartment door.

"Got a moment, Milo?" Matt asked.

"Not you guys again," he replied sadly.

"We have a few more questions. Then we'll be on our way."

Milo shrugged and led us into his messy living room. He didn't ask us to sit down, but we plopped down on his couch, pushing magazines out of the way. When Milo saw that his remaining standing was not encouraging us to hurry and leave, he sat in his recliner. The table beside it was covered with dirty laundry.

"You lied to us about your hospital stay," Matt said, coming out swinging.

"I did not!"

"Your records are not in the system."

"My records are confidential. You have no access to them."

"We know you weren't admitted. So, let's skip all the BS and speak honestly. We've discovered your relationship with Claire had become very rocky. Some claim it was abusive."

"Nonsense!"

"The police were called to your house more than once."

"Claire overreacted. I never touched her, and she didn't file any charges."

"You knew she was having an affair with Levings. That couldn't have made you happy."

Milo's face grew red. He struggled to regain his composure. "She broke off the affair."

"After you two separated, and the damage had already been done."

"I've already told you I had nothing to do with her death, if that's what you're implying." He sounded more weary than angry.

"You were still married to her. You're getting her family fortune, which could fund years of future research."

"I can get funding in other ways. I would never kill her for money. Or because of her affair."

I stood. "Mind if I grab a glass of water?"

"There's bottled water in the fridge," Milo replied.

"Anyone else want water?" I asked.

The men ignored me as they frowned at each other.

When I walked past him on my way to the kitchen, I sprinkled my truth-spell dust on his feet unnoticed. Though I couldn't be sure his extreme intelligence wouldn't defeat the spell, I had to try anyway. I silently chanted the incantation while in the kitchen, then returned to the sofa, glancing at Milo to see if he was enchanted yet.

He appeared to be hot and sweaty, not enchanted. I touched the Red Dragon talisman in my pocket and put more energy into the spell, pushing it into Milo. His face became animated and eyes glassy.

"Milo," I said in a soothing voice, "you'll know you'll feel much better if you tell the truth about Claire's death. Maybe you didn't intend to kill her. Maybe you brought the worm to her as a gift, a peace offering, an act of endearment. Could that be the case?"

"No. A Mongolian Death Worm isn't the kind of gift you leave in someone's bedroom like jewelry or a box of chocolates." He stared at me with sincerity. "Though it *would* make a delightful gift if presented properly."

"Okay, I'll keep that in mind for your next birthday."

He didn't notice my sarcasm. "Would you? That would be the best!"

Movement caught my eye. It had been too slight and brief to identify.

"It's okay to admit you were angry at Claire," I said, refusing to abandon this line of questioning.

"Yes, I was angry at Claire. She never truly supported me when I changed my career to cryptozoology."

"Can you blame her?" Matt interjected. He snapped his mouth shut when I glared at him for disturbing my connection with the spell's subject.

"I walked away from a high-paying job in bioengineering," Milo continued. "But I had no passion for it. This," he gestured to the specimens in his bookcase, "is what fascinates me."

Something moved again. It was the dirty clothes on the table next to him. But even the stinkiest socks and shirts can't move on their own.

"Then Claire cheated on me," Milo continued. "Not with her personal trainer or someone like that, but with my professional rival. For me, the worst person in the entire world for her to have an affair with."

The dirty clothes moved again. There had to be a mouse crawling around in there. I was about to alert Milo when I discovered it wasn't a mouse at all.

The head of a death worm emerged from a pair of boxer shorts and pointed its gaping mouth with dripping teeth at Milo's head.

CHAPTER 19
BOOKWORMS

Milo noticed my horrified stare and turned, ending up face to face with the death worm right beside him. Instead of being scared, he smiled. Yes, he actually smiled.

"My God," he breathed. "A death worm, at last. You incredible creature! I've given my life's work to—"

A jet of venom shot from the worm's mouth, splattering over Milo's face. Milo screamed as the pain of the acidic burning told him that this wasn't the happy encounter he had thought it would be.

Matt and I screamed at the same time and instinctively jerked backwards away from the worm, sending the sofa falling backwards. We hit the floor, cushioned by the sofa's backrest. We scrambled upright and peered over the wall created by the sofa's seat. Milo was slumped sideways in his chair with the worm on top of him.

The worm was munching on Milo.

"Cast your spell," Matt whispered so the worm wouldn't hear him, though the worm was preoccupied at the moment.

"I'm working on it."

As quickly as I could, I cast my Arctic-chill spell, mumbling the incantation with numb lips and grasping the Red Dragon talisman in my pocket with a trembling hand. I sent the magic to the worm, and it almost instantly stopped moving and dropped to the floor.

"I'm calling nine-one-one," Matt said. He told the operator it was a poisoning, "maybe fatal."

"We have to get the worm out of here before the paramedics arrive," I told him. "Get the empty wooden box I found in the bedroom when we searched the place."

I hurried to Milo. I couldn't check his carotid artery for a pulse because his face and neck were covered with venom, so I tried his wrist. There was no pulse, and he wasn't breathing. The venom had overcome him.

"He's dead," I said in a flat voice.

Matt returned to the living room with the box, and I searched for a tool to pick up the worm. The best I could do was a large pair of salad tongs from the kitchen. Matt smirked ironically when he saw me use them to transfer the worm into the box.

I called the Society's emergency number, leaving a message that we needed a cryptid extraction ASAP. Red and white strobe lights seeped through the window blinds from the parking lot as the ambulance arrived.

"Let's get out of here," I said.

Matt helped me carry the box out the back door. The goblin wearing white overalls stood there, a smile on his hairy face.

"I'll take that. Thank you," Frankie said.

"How did you get here so fast?" Matt asked.

Frankie didn't answer before hurrying away with the box. I had known he wouldn't.

"I think Levings was responsible for this," I said.

"Me, too."

"It's time to nail him to the wall."

"WE NEED to interview more members of the Mongolian expedition," Matt said during our drive back to Jellyfish Beach. "One of them might admit that a worm was actually captured and Levings brought it home."

"That would be great. Because as it stands now, I'm pretty sure Milo didn't kill Claire. But we can't rule him out one hundred percent."

"Milo showed no signs that he found the worm and planted it to kill Claire."

"True," I admitted. "And we can assume Milo was attacked by one of the worm's offspring that was captured on the beach. But I guess anyone could have killed Milo, assuming they could capture a worm."

"You're overthinking this," Matt replied. "Who else would have a motive to kill Milo other than Levings? Levings killed Claire because he was angry she broke off their affair. He killed Milo because of . . . professional rivalry?"

"Or because of the book Milo was writing. Milo's book purported to prove the Mongolian Death Worm existed, based on the molted skin, while exposing Levings as a fraud who profited from perpetuating the worm legend. Levings is writing a book, too. But his book claims *he* discovered new evidence that the worm really exists. It looked like his book was further along than Milo's. If Milo died, he wouldn't finish his book, and Levings's book wouldn't have any competition or damning criticism. Ironically, if the worms keep reproducing and the public finds out about them, both books will be irrelevant. The death worm would no longer be a fascinating cryptid. Just a dangerous invasive species."

Matt nodded. "True. The Cryptid Society aren't the only folks who need to get rid of the worms."

Unexpected feelings of guilt flooded me. "Did we contribute to Milo's death?"

"How?"

"By telling Levings that Milo was alive and well and back in America, writing a book about the death worm."

"Don't be ridiculous," Matt said. "Levings would have found out. Maybe he already knew Milo was here. Milo's neighbor said that someone resembling Zora was scoping out Milo's apartment. And he would have heard from his publisher that Milo had a book deal."

"Thanks for trying to make me feel better, but it's not working."

"Sorry."

"It doesn't matter now. We need to find evidence tying Levings to Claire's and Milo's deaths. Or at least one of them. If he was the one who planted the worms, I'm obligated to inform the Society."

"I think you should go to the police first, if the evidence is good enough."

"That's not what I was told to do," I insisted.

"What if the Society harmed Levings? It would be like vigilante justice. Could you live with yourself?"

I didn't answer his question because I didn't know the answer. "Let's find some evidence and take it from there."

CHAD PENNYWICK WAS a skinny man with thinning hair and an English accent. He was famous for short, documentary-style videos of alleged paranormal activity and cryptid sightings. Most of his videos went viral. He had been hired by Milo and Levings to accompany the expedition to Mongolia and capture video that generated publicity. Because the team never found a worm, only the molted skin, Chad's videos from Mongolia weren't exactly a big hit on social media.

We met with him in his Orlando office as he sat in front of a giant monitor, working with video-editing software. We broke the news about Milo's death, and revealed Claire's true cause of death, but said nothing about the worms proliferating on the beach.

He assured us a worm was never found while he was on the expedition, but added that he left early, not long after Milo disappeared, because of another assignment back in America. He conceded that a worm could have been captured after he departed without anyone telling him about it.

"A worm in Jellyfish Beach!" he said with excitement. "I

want to get some video of it. Then, I hope it dies and is never captured."

I was shocked that he felt this way. "Why?"

"Levings would be thrilled to have the worm. He could go on speaking tours across the world showing it off." Chad pushed his eyeglasses higher up his nose. "But for me, the best outcome would be to get footage of it, yet the worm is never captured. That would enhance the allure of the legend, and my videos would be absolute sensations."

"I see." I told him my theory that his scenario would help the success of Levings's soon-to-be-published book.

"Yes," he replied. "If Levings possessed a worm, he would need to revise his book. Or trash it and write a new one."

"What is better for Levings's career?" Matt asked. "To capture a worm or not?"

Chad pondered this for a moment. "If he had a worm, he would be momentarily famous, but that would soon fade, and he would need to choose a different cryptid to hype. His best option would be to publicize new evidence that the worm exists while continuing to search for it."

"But would he give up a worm if he had one?" I asked.

"Perhaps. But only after hiring me to shoot great footage of it. Why?"

"If he placed a worm in the Fusseldink's home to kill Claire, he must have known there would be a good chance it would escape and he wouldn't be able to find it again."

Chad stared at me. "You think Levings killed Claire Fusseldink?"

"Possibly. And maybe Milo, too. What do you think, Chad?" I explained that Levings had been involved with Claire.

"I didn't know that. I can't speak to whether he would kill her. Killing Milo, though, wouldn't surprise me. The two argued endlessly during the expedition before Milo disappeared."

"What if Levings had more than one worm?" Matt asked. "Let's say he found a worm in Mongolia, and it reproduced parthenogenetically. Then, he would have a spare and could afford to lose the one he planted to kill Claire. The worm reproduced again, giving him another spare to use to kill Milo."

"I like your theory," I said.

"I do, as well," Chad said. "Perhaps the best strategy of all for Levings would be to capture a worm and keep it secret. He could then take photos and videos of it, pretending that he saw it in the wild, and release the evidence in dribs and drabs. They would go instantly viral, and he could sustain his fame for years."

"Your theory is my favorite," I said.

"Mine, too," said Matt.

"Are you still in touch with Levings?" I asked Chad.

"We exchange emails regularly. I'm hoping for another assignment from him."

"Will you promise to keep our chat secret and to let us know if you hear anything new from him about death worms?" I asked, slipping Chad five $100 bills. Matt, as a principled reporter, would not offer bribes, but his tabloid-news rivals had great success with the tactic. So, I had dipped into my savings, hoping the Society would reimburse me.

Chad snatched the cash. "I most certainly will. I'll even ask Levings some probing questions for you."

"Just don't be too obvious," Matt added.

"I've never been known for subtlety, but I can manage it."

I DROVE Matt to his bungalow, and he invited me to stay for dinner.

"I have fresh snapper I caught early this morning," he said with an innocent grin. "And plenty of Pino Grigio. You deserve a relaxing evening."

"The cats and iguana need to be fed."

"No harm if they eat late."

The thought of him cooking dinner for me was appealing. As was the possibility of a bit of romance. Only a little, mind you.

However, my mood was shattered by the high-pitched buzzing in my head.

"The wards at my house just went off," I said. "Someone's trespassing. Possibly breaking in. I don't think it's Ruth."

"Report it to the police. Say your alarm system went off."

"Shortle knows I don't have an alarm. And you realize as well as I do that the intruder is more likely to be supernatural than a common criminal. I need to drive home now."

"I'm coming with you."

I resisted the urge to go too far above the speed limit, and my stomach was in knots by the time we rolled down my quiet, middle-class suburban street. Darkness had fallen, but I recognized the few cars parked along the curb. Except for one—a green vintage sports car sitting two houses from mine.

I passed my house slowly, looking for anyone lurking

outside. There was no one visible from the street. My front porch light was on, as intended, as well as the lamp in the living room that I kept on a timer. A cardboard box sat on the porch in front of the door. It was probably the pungi Dr. Hooey had promised to send me. It had arrived almost as fast as a gewgaw bought on the internet.

I drove around the cul-de-sac and parked in front of a neighbor's house. Matt and I walked silently to my house, keeping to the shadows, which were abundant because the nearest streetlamp was far up the street.

We had no weapons except for my immobility spell. I had prepared it halfway to save time in case I needed to use it quickly. I gestured to Matt that he should go around the right side of the house, and I would circle around the left, past my one-car garage. There were more places to hide along the route I was taking.

When I crept past the half-open window on the side of the garage, a little green hand reached out and waved at me. It was Tony's iguana foreleg. He was still enchanted by Ruth's spell that had silenced him, so all he could do was point frantically at the jacaranda bush in the rear corner of the house.

I approached the bush as quietly as I could, and when I neared it, I cast a second spell I had also prepared halfway. An orb of dazzling white light appeared, floating above the bush. From between the leaves and the trumpet-shaped blue flowers gleamed white skin and dyed blonde hair.

The trespasser hiding behind the bush was Zora.

CHAPTER 20

THAT HORRID WOMAN

"Good evening, Zora," I said. "What a pleasant surprise."

She flexed her leg muscles, preparing to burst from behind the bush and escape, but I sent my immobility spell to stop her. Doing so drained the energy from my glowing orb, which went dark and disappeared. My eyes adjusted to the almost total darkness, and I watched her carefully to make sure she couldn't move.

Footsteps approached from the backyard, and Matt arrived, shining a flashlight at Zora. "Wow. It's Zora. Why am I not surprised?"

"Don't shine that light in my eyes," Zora said.

"Well, Missy, I found these stuck to your windows." He handed me three tiny electronic boxes. "Listening devices that can monitor a room, even when placed on the outside of windows."

"You're spying on us, Zora," I said. "Why would you do that?"

"Just following orders."

"From Levings?"

She didn't answer, but I knew I was correct.

"Why didn't you leave before I got here?" I asked.

"I was told to see if you came home alone." Her eyes moved to Matt, the only part of her beside her mouth, heart, and lungs that could move while under my spell. "Or if your partner here is your domestic partner."

"Absolutely not!"

"You don't have to be so adamant," Matt complained.

"What did you do to me?" Zora asked. "Why can't I move?"

"It's a form of hypnosis," I lied. "It won't hurt you. If you answer my questions honestly, I'll make it wear off."

Matt tugged me to him and whispered in my ear, "Aren't you going to use your truth spell?"

"That and the immobility spell require too much magical energy," I whispered back. "I can only maintain one at a time."

I returned to my spot at the jacaranda bush. "Why is Dr. Levings surveilling me?"

"Why can't I move? Stop what you're doing," Zora pleaded. "This isn't hypnosis; it's magic or something."

"It's hypnosis."

"You're a witch, aren't you?"

"There's no such thing. Now answer my question. Why is Dr. Levings surveilling me?"

She hesitated before answering. "You've been asking him too many questions. He doesn't trust you."

“Is the green car parked on the street his?”

“Yes.”

“He made you bug my home. It’s not about distrusting me. He fears me. He’s afraid I know what he’s done. Correct?”

“No. He’s done nothing wrong.”

“He had an affair with Milo’s wife. Don’t try to deny it.”

This upset her. She struggled with her emotions, made worse by being physically frozen in place. “The affair ended long before she died. Don’t you dare accuse Dr. Levings of killing that horrid woman!”

“You keep calling her horrid.”

“Because she was materialistic and selfish. And she started the affair, not Dr. Levings. I don’t blame Milo for killing her.”

“What makes you think he killed her? Do you have any proof?”

“He was a petty, vindictive man with a gigantic ego. He couldn’t bear the thought of his wife being with his rival.”

“Do you have any proof?”

“No. But I think Milo found a death worm and brought it home.”

“Did you know he left the expedition early and wasn’t missing in the desert?”

She paused. “Yes.”

“How do you know?”

“Why are you asking me all these questions? Why am I paralyzed like this? It’s freaking me out! Please help me!”

“Answer my questions, and we’ll get you back to normal,” I said, putting more kindness into my voice. “Tell us what we want to know, and you can leave.”

With my nursing background, making someone feel uncomfortable made me feel, well, terrible. But we needed answers, and I believed I would make more progress with Zora than Matt, being an aggressive man, would. Of course, Zora had been accustomed to dealing with overbearing men.

"Dr. Levings ordered me to snoop around Milo's apartment."

"Did you actually break in?"

"Yes." She sounded ashamed. "I was told to check on the progress of Milo's book. He's old-school and prints out his manuscript chapter by chapter. Dr. Levings is concerned that Milo's book will contradict his. But Milo seems to be a slower writer. Dr. Levings should be able to publish his own book first."

"You speak of Milo in the present tense. Why?"

"What are you talking about?"

"Milo is dead."

Zora's face was too frozen to form expressions. I couldn't tell if she was surprised.

"Are you sure? What—what happened?"

I paused and fed more energy into the immobility spell before taking a different line of questioning. "You're Dr. Levings's research assistant, right?"

"More like his teaching assistant. He does his own research, except for the occasional field expedition."

"Why do you act like he's a Mafia boss? Breaking into his rival's apartment and spying on me are not part of your job description."

She was flustered. "They are now."

"Can't you just tell him no—that you won't do that?"

"Listen, I admire the man. He's my mentor, my hero. I would do anything for him."

Something in her tone went beyond pure admiration.

"Do you fancy Dr. Levings?" I asked.

My spell didn't prevent Zora from blushing, which was obvious even in the moonlight. "I care about him."

"Do you love him?"

"No." Her mood turned dark. "Not after he had a fling with that horrid woman."

"Did you ever have a fling with him?"

"That's none of your business!"

"Sorry to offend you," I said sarcastically. "It almost sounds as if he dumped you for Claire."

"I'm not talking to you anymore. Let me go."

I caught Matt's eye and nodded to him. It was his turn to play bad cop.

"Zora," he said aggressively, leaning over the bush so his face was close to hers. "Did you put the worm in Claire Fusseldink's bedroom?"

"No, I would never do something like that. I told you I believe Milo did it."

"Are you responsible for Milo's death?"

"Of course not!"

"Do you believe Dr. Levings is to blame for their deaths?"

She whimpered. "He couldn't be. That's crazy."

"Stop trying to protect him. I'm not asking if you have proof. Just tell me if you have any suspicion at all that he did it."

“I don’t know. Maybe. He’s not a killer, he’s not. But I don’t know. Sometimes people are pushed too far by their emotions.”

“Break the immobility spell,” Matt whispered in my ear. “I’ll restrain her. Cast the truth spell on her with all the energy you have.”

Matt went behind the jacaranda bush and wrapped his arms around Zora, then nodded to me.

I broke the immobility spell, and Zora collapsed into Matt’s arms. Quickly diverting my energy to building the truth spell, I cast it upon Zora and reached over the bush to sprinkle the powder on her feet.

“Is Dr. Levings responsible for the deaths of the Fusseldinks?” I asked sternly.

She replied with an animal-like roar, stomped on Matt’s feet, and elbowed him in the gut. As he struggled to constrain her frenzied writhing, Zora head-butted him in the nose.

She almost knocked me down as she burst from behind the bush and fled to Levings’s car. Before I could cast another spell to stop her, the car roared to life and, with a screech of tires, rocketed away down the street.

“Tell Dr. Levings to stop spying on me,” I halfheartedly called out after her.

“I think Levings is our guy,” Matt said, blood dripping from his nose. “Do you?”

I nodded. “I take it you weren’t on the wrestling team in school.”

He ignored my comment. “You should tell Shortle about Levings.”

“I’ve already said that I’m obligated to report to the Society first.”

"Indeed, you are," said Mrs. Lupis. She and her partner had mysteriously appeared in my driveway, looking out of place in their gray suits and black attaché cases.

"Our justice department needs to set the record straight before the suspect is turned over to the police," Mr. Lopez said. "Let's go inside and review your evidence."

"Wait a minute," I said. "How can I be sure the Society won't harm or kill Levings?"

"We're not animals," Mrs. Lupis said, affronted.

"But you're not human, either."

"That's a fact in our favor," Mr. Lopez said. "Humans don't have a history of being humane with your justice systems."

"Most of the time, we are."

My handlers snickered as they followed me inside.

My phone vibrated on my nightstand from an incoming text. It was long before dawn. Bubba and Brenda burrowed beneath my comforter. When I reached for my phone, I found an iguana lying beside it. Tony wasn't supposed to sleep in my bedroom, but I'd been cutting him some slack in sympathy for his suffering under Ruth's spell.

The text was from Mrs. Lupis:

The Society's agents arrived at Dr. Levings's house just as the police were taking him away. Find out what you can.

I texted back that I would. Maybe this was better, I thought, that the police arrested Levings before the Society got their hands on him.

"No, we didn't arrest him," Detective Shortle said to Matt and me in the lobby of the police department. "He's a person of interest in several recent deaths."

"Several?" I asked. "We think he's guilty of killing Claire and Milo Fusseldink."

"If he's responsible for releasing the so-called death worms, he's also guilty of negligent homicide for the deaths of the people on the beach and the golfer. I doubt he'll be charged for those, however. We're trying to keep the public from knowing about the worms before we eradicate the problem. If the information went public, it would be devastating to our tourism business."

"The world's greatest understatement," Matt murmured. "Do you really believe you can keep the worms a secret?"

"Animal Control personnel will capture them soon. I'm confident of that."

Matt and I exchanged glances. I didn't share Shortle's confidence that the city could capture the worms. But if they caught even one of them, it would pose a major problem for the Cryptid Society because they wanted the worm to keep its cryptid status as a creature only known in legend.

Time to change the subject. "Has Levings been taken into custody?" I asked.

"No, just questioned. We've already sent him home."

"What do you think? Is he guilty?"

Shortle smiled. "You know I can't discuss that with you."

"I know. But I had to try."

As soon as Matt and I left the building, I texted Mrs. Lupis:

Levings's status is a person of interest. He is not under arrest. He has been interrogated and released.

Several minutes later, Mrs. Lupis replied:

Correction: Levings's status is deceased. Our agents just found his body in his home.

CHAPTER 21

DEATH BY DEATH WORM

Mrs. Lupis texted me Levings's home address, and Matt and I hurried along Alligator Alley to the crime scene, which was in a tidy suburb near the university. I had asked Mrs. Lupis to hold off reporting the death to the police to allow time for us to examine the scene before the professionals arrived.

Was this delay breaking the law? Bending the law? Well, we dealt with a world that bent the laws of logic, so I figured we could bend the laws of humans. In fact, I wasn't even certain Mrs. Lupis would have notified human law enforcement if I hadn't mentioned it.

When we arrived at Levings's house, it was still dark out. The garage door was closed, so I assumed the victim's car was parked in there since no car was in the driveway or at the curb. The front door was unlocked, so we let ourselves in and found my handlers standing in the living room.

"Where are the justice agents?" I asked.

"They just left," Mr. Lopez said. "They're not very sociable. The stiff's in the master bedroom, by the way."

In the bedroom, I found exactly what I had been expecting: Levings dead on the floor, lying face up with a huge grin on his acid-burned face. Yet another death by death worm.

Matt peered cautiously under the bed. "Do you think the worm is still around?"

"I don't know. Watch your step. I'm gathering energies for my Arctic-freeze spell, just in case we find the worm. Let's check all the windows and doors to see if there's an escape route."

All the windows in the bedroom and attached bath were closed, as was the case throughout the house. In the rear of the one-story home was a mudroom with laundry machines. An exterior door was slightly open, leaving a gap of a few inches.

"I bet the worm left the house here," Matt said. "Whoever brought the worm to the house made sure it wouldn't be trapped inside."

"They might not have brought the worm here at all," I said. "I noticed something when I was checking the windows in the family room. Follow me."

We returned to the room where, in most houses, a giant TV and seating areas would be. Levings had created a library instead, complete with a fireplace. On a table beside one of the many built-in bookcases was a large glass terrarium. Inside was a deep layer of sand with a small rock on top of it. A section of an underground burrow was visible where it met the glass.

"Wow," Matt said. "Looks like he kept a worm here as a pet."

"A pet that killed him. Look, the terrarium cover has been left open."

"Someone must have opened it so the worm would escape and attack Levings. He wouldn't be so stupid as to leave it open by accident, right?"

"That could have happened," I said, hoping there wasn't a second worm beneath the sand about to pop out and attack us. "But the fact that the mudroom door was open probably means someone else opened the tank as well as the door to allow the worm to flee."

"What if they just wanted to free the worm and didn't know it would attack Levings?"

"Could be. But if they understood anything about this species, they would know it's very aggressive and hungry for meat. Let's make one more pass through the house to make sure the worm isn't still inside."

We carefully inspected each room, peering beneath furniture, and looking in drawers, cabinets, and closets. Passing through the living room again, we explained to Mrs. Lupis and Mr. Lopez what we were doing. They turned pale and stepped onto the coffee table. The garage was the scariest place, with so many places for a death worm to hide, from Levings's car to the metal shelving units, to the bags and fertilizer and mulch stacked on the floor.

"Who do you think released the worm?" Matt asked as he shifted a bag of cypress mulch to look for holes.

"Someone who knew he kept a worm here. Someone who knew he'd been taken in for questioning and was afraid of what he would say. A person who has strong, conflicted feelings about Levings."

"Zora?"

"Yep," I replied. "I still believe we're correct in guessing that Levings was behind the deaths of Claire and Milo. He had plenty of motives and obviously had access to worms. I think Zora killed him out of resentment. He treated her like a slave and had an affair that he didn't hide from her, even though she was in love with him. They probably had a fling of their own before Levings switched to Claire's bed."

"You think she was worried about Levings being questioned by the police?"

"I believe Levings was behind the killings, but I would bet that Zora did the dirty work for him. You heard her admit she regularly broke into Milo's apartment on Levings's orders. The last time she did it, she probably left a worm there. She did the same in Claire's bedroom."

"You could be right. But we have no proof."

"We'll need to find and restrain her. Then, I'll use my truth spell on her while we shoot video of her confession. But first, we need to find this missing worm."

We used a side door to exit the garage and swept our flashlights across the lawn.

"We're miles from the beach," Matt said. "Could a worm even survive out here without sand?"

"Don't forget, beneath this beautiful grass, the land is mostly sandy."

"But would the worm sense there's sand under the sod?"

"I don't know. We've got to find it, though. We can't leave it out here in suburbia and allow it to kill someone else. There must be some exposed sand nearby."

"Like a sandbox? The thought of a kid playing in it is horrifying."

I needed a magical means of surveying the neighborhood. A familiar trilling owl call from an oak tree in the backyard gave me an idea. I conjured an attraction spell, an ancient spell long used to arouse interest in someone you had a crush on. You could use it on animals, too, making them curious about you or, if you're not careful, make them want to eat you.

The Eastern Screech-Owl flew toward me and perched on a rain gutter just above me. Now that he was in proximity, I locked eyes with him, pumped more energy into my spell, and established a mental connection with him. I encouraged his urge for hunting rodents. And, most importantly, empowered myself to see through his eyes with magic.

He flew in lazy circles over Levings's yard, then expanded the radius of his circle. With the owl's fantastic night vision, I saw the neighbors' properties in perfect detail.

The owl flew over what I was looking for in the property two houses away: a backyard beach-volleyball court covered with sand.

"Bingo," I said. "A beach-volleyball court."

I sent a wave of gratitude to the owl and released him from my spell.

"You mean, a court with trucked-in sand?" Matt asked.

"Yeah. Two doors down. Let me grab something from my car, and we'll go check out the sand."

When I returned with my gifted pungi in hand, Matt stared at it in disbelief. "What the heck is that?"

"A pungi, of course."

"Of course. What the heck is a pungi? Some kind of musical instrument?"

"Obviously. A reed flute made from a gourd."

"Obviously. I'm a big fan of Beethoven's Pungi Concerto Number One."

"It's what snake charmers in India use with cobras. Dr. Hooey said it might work with death worms, too. The creatures respond to the vibrations."

"And they'll come to the surface?"

"That's what Dr. Hooey believes."

"It's worth a try. We don't want to allow the worm to remain free in suburbia and multiply."

"Let's go," I said. "We have to be careful sneaking into the family's backyard."

We walked down the street to the house in question. The eastern sky showed a hint of dawn, but there weren't any lights on in the house that we could see. The property didn't have a fence, only a dense wall of areca palms providing privacy from neighbors. We slipped through the shadows past the side of the house into the large backyard.

Next to the swimming pool was the volleyball court I had seen through the owl's eyes, the sand shining white in the moonlight. The surface of the sand on both sides of the net was disturbed, suggesting a lot of intense play. And perhaps a burrowing worm. We stood at the edge of the sand.

"I watched a video on how to play this thing," I said, bringing the gourd flute to my lips. "But I don't know any songs. Don't criticize my musical talent. It's the vibrations that matter."

I blew on the instrument with the proper technique to

make the reed vibrate. The tone was reminiscent of music from India, but the tune was horrible. I wasn't sure how loudly I should play; I wanted the worm to feel it but didn't want the sleeping residents to hear.

Matt looked at me with dismay at my travesty of music, then turned his attention to the sand, looking for movement. Was it my imagination, or was the sand shifting a bit to our right?

A door opened behind us, and a sleepy male voice shouted, "What are you doing in my yard?"

It was a large man with an enormous belly, wearing nothing but shorts.

"Animal Control," Matt was quick to respond. "We're trying to catch an invasive reptile."

I continued playing the pungi, more certain that I had seen sand shifting.

"You can't come onto my property without my permission," the man growled. He pulled a handgun from the back of his shorts and aimed it at us. "Get out of here before I blow you away. And stop that ugly music!"

I finally stopped playing. "This is a pungi from the Indian subcontinent. It can make beautiful music if only I could get the hang of it."

The death worm chose that inconvenient moment to pop up, extending vertically from the sand like a hypnotized cobra in front of a snake charmer.

"Holy moly!" The homeowner exclaimed. "What the heck is that thing?"

A floodlight came on, making the volleyball court look as if it were in daylight.

With the music stopped and the light shining in its eyes, the worm appeared to be furious at our presence. It opened its giant round mouth with jagged teeth dripping in slime.

"Step back!" I warned Matt.

The worm sent a geyser of venom toward us. It fell short, though drops of it spattered against Matt's calves beneath his shorts.

Matt hissed in pain.

Two gunshots shattered the night. Puffs of sand flew in the air on either side of the worm. The creature began to slide back into its burrow until two more shots were fired and the worm exploded in a shower of gore.

"That's one less worm I have to catch," I muttered.

"My skin is burning," Matt said. "But I feel great!"

"You two are next if you don't leave now," the homeowner said.

By this time, lights were on in his house, as well as his neighbors' homes.

"We'll be on our way," I said, sidestepping carefully in the direction from which we had come. I hoped to get out of here alive and before the police showed up.

Then, to my surprise, two individuals strolled around the house into the backyard. Mrs. Lupis and Mr. Lopez. They gave me a little wave, completely unperturbed by the gunfire mere seconds ago.

"*More* people in my backyard?" the homeowner asked furiously. "You'd better be cops or I'll shoot you under the Stand Your Ground law."

"You could say we're a form of law enforcement," Mr. Lopez said with a smirk. He flashed a badge at the man and headed straight for the volleyball court to stare at the remains of the worm. Pulling a plastic leaf bag from his attaché case, he used his foot to push the worm pieces into it.

"You could also say we're mental therapists," said Mrs. Lupis to the man. "We're here to wipe away your traumatic memories of tonight so you won't be troubled."

"What are you talking—"

She raised her right arm, palm facing the homeowner. His face went blank, and he swayed on his feet as if he were about to pass out.

"Time to leave." Mrs. Lupis gestured for Matt and me to follow her and her partner from the backyard to the street.

"How did you know what happened here?" I asked, forgetting that my question was a waste of time.

"We sensed you were having a worm encounter," Mr. Lopez said. "Frankie was on his way here before we realized the worm was deceased."

"Of course. That makes perfect sense. Wait, where are you going?" I asked when they got into the backseat of my car, uninvited.

"We're going with you to the new suspect's home. We understand you've had a breakthrough in the murder cases."

"Not a breakthrough," I replied. "Just a strong hunch that Zora is responsible for the death of Dr. Levings. And might have been an accessory to the other deaths."

"Also, our other suspects are all dead now," Matt added. "It's a process of elimination."

"A very slow process," Mrs. Lupis said. "But what else could we expect of humans? Do you know where Zora lives?"

"Yeah. We staked it out once before," I said, driving slowly out of the neighborhood.

"We did, too," Mr. Lopez said. "It's on the other side of town, so you'd best pick up your speed."

The long drive was helpful for Zora, because it turned out she was expecting us.

CHAPTER 22

SWAMP APE APARTMENTS

When we arrived at Zora's apartment complex, we had a plan worked out. My handlers described in great detail the layout of the apartment complex where many graduate students at the university lived. The plan was for Mrs. Lupis and Mr. Lopez to block Zora's escape routes, while Matt and I broke in through the front door and captured her in bed. It was just past dawn—early enough that we assumed she would still be asleep.

"What if she's not in her apartment?" Matt asked. "She's been through a lot of stress and might not be able to sleep."

"In that case, I'll use one of her possessions to cast a locator spell to find her," I replied. I mentioned that I also had a sleep spell queued up. It would be the best way to capture her quietly. We would interrogate her after we'd taken her elsewhere from her apartment.

"We hope that won't be necessary," Mr. Lopez said from my backseat.

"I want to question her before the justice agents do."

"No need for that. The agents are on their way to take the subject into custody."

I gave my handlers a stern stare in the rearview mirror. "I wouldn't feel right handing her over to them without being certain of her guilt."

My handlers didn't reply. They merely smiled grimly.

"It's coming up on the right," Mrs. Lupis said.

The complex was called the Swamp Ape Apartments, a name that would delight the cryptozoological students while seeming hokey to the other residents. There was an elegant carving on the complex's wooden sign of the Sasquatch-like cryptid, believed to live in this region of Florida.

The parking lot was well lit, and I found a spot close to Building A, where Zora lived in Unit 207.

"The apartment has a balcony facing the swimming pool," Mrs. Lupis said. "Mr. Lopez will be stationed beneath the balcony in case she jumps. I'll be waiting at the top of the stairs beside the elevator in case she escapes from the front of her apartment." She caught my eye. "Ideally, she will not escape."

"She won't," I said with false certainty.

Matt and I walked down the breezeway to 207. The building was completely silent at this hour, though the sun had already risen. When we reached Zora's door, I cast a quick spell to heighten my senses and pressed my ear against the door. Her apartment was silent.

Next, I cast an unlocking spell to get us through the door. It took a while to unlock both the deadbolt and the lock in the door handle. While I was doing it, Matt pulled a taser from his pocket.

"You're going to use *that*?" I asked after I had completed the unlocking. "That's cruel."

"It's not cruel if she has a gun. And in Florida, that's a strong possibility. I don't have one. This is my only weapon for defending myself. I don't have magic like you."

"Magic can't stop everyone," I muttered, hoping Zora wouldn't be one it didn't.

We entered the dark apartment and closed the door behind us, pausing while our eyes adjusted. It was a generic, contemporary apartment with a door to the bedroom on the living room wall. I assumed it wouldn't be locked. I gathered my energies and completed casting a sleep spell that would knock Zora out as soon as I had her in my sight.

I looked at Matt. He nodded to show that he was ready. I grasped the doorknob and turned it slightly. It was indeed unlocked. Taking a deep breath, I pushed the door quietly—

It flew open, and a giant creature barreled out of the bedroom, knocking Matt and me to the floor. The creature emitted an ear-piercing shriek.

Matt's taser flew from his hand and bounced away across the floor. Lying on my back, I tried to send my sleep spell, but the shock of the ambush had thrown off my concentration and dispersed the magical energies I had amassed.

"I sensed you were coming," Zora said in a hoarse voice. "Your questioning of me earlier was not subtle. You came here to blame me for things I didn't do."

My mouth dropped open when I realized she wasn't in human form. Yes, her head, arms, and upper torso were normal, but the rest of her was the body of a giant eagle: feathers, wings, talons, and all. It made her almost too tall to pass through the doorway. She had to duck her head as she emerged and tossed Matt into the kitchen with one talon.

She was a harpy, a monster from Greek mythology. A cryptid of the ancient world.

"You, witch, are going for a swim in the Gulf. Several miles out. Your boyfriend, too. They'll find your bodies when you wash ashore in a day or two."

I tried again to cast the sleep spell, but it was too late. The harpy flapped her enormous eagle wings and knocked me into the wall along with a tornado of flying bric-à-brac. Matt was on his knees, searching for his taser on the floor.

"Matt, get out of here!" I shouted.

"I'm not leaving you behind."

Zora turned her human head toward him.

"Go now, Matt! I need you to be alive."

The harpy moved toward him, and he finally jumped to his feet and sprinted from the apartment.

Zora cursed after she failed to grab Matt in time. She returned her attention to me, strutting over and seizing my chest and pelvis in her talons. The grip was so strong that I could barely breathe. With a human arm, she pulled my phone from my pocket and tossed it under the sofa.

She awkwardly traveled to her bedroom, half flying and half hopping—each hop crushing me with her weight. Her human arms opened a sliding-glass door leading to a balcony where she took flight, swooping over a courtyard, a swimming pool, and Mr. Lopez looking up at us, mouth agape, utterly useless for rescuing me.

Zora flew above the sprawl of Fort Myers and its suburbs. My struggle to breathe was replaced by the fear of being dropped from this height. We crossed the shimmering dark green of Estero Bay and the narrow strip of Fort Myers Beach. Then we were above the purple expanse of the Gulf.

My mind finally moved from the initial physical panic of being caught like a mouse by an eagle to the existential fear that my life would be over soon if I didn't come up with a plan.

"Don't even think of using a spell on me," Zora shouted above the wind and her flapping wings. "I'll drop you the instant I feel magic."

"You're going to drop me anyway," I shouted back. "Why don't you just do it now and put me out of my misery?"

"We're too close to shore. Fishing boats could rescue you."

I hadn't been able to think of a spell that would disable her without her crashing and killing me. If I couldn't use magic, I would try persuasion.

"There's no point in killing me. My friend is a witness. And your secrets are already known by the Friends of Cryptids Society."

"I don't care. You're wrong about me, and no one will catch me. After I drop you, I'm going to fly to Mexico or Central America."

"The Society will find you for sure. They have agents everywhere in the Americas. And how are you going to survive? Your eagle body doesn't have pockets for credit cards. And if you shift back to human form, you'll be naked."

"Don't worry about me."

"I do worry about you," I said with sincerity. Though, truth be told, I was more worried about myself at the moment. "The Cryptids Society can help you now that you've revealed yourself as a harpy. Because you're not human, they can protect you from the human justice system."

"I'm innocent. Why do I need protection?"

"Because you don't look innocent at all. There's lots of circumstantial evidence tying you to the deaths of Claire, Milo, and Levings. You can say you're innocent all you want, but a jury will still convict you. You need our protection."

I could no longer see the land behind us or any boats. There was nothing but open water below.

Zora flapped her wings harder, and we rose higher.

"Why are we going higher?" I asked.

"I've decided to be merciful. A longer fall means you'll be killed or knocked unconscious when you hit the water. You won't suffer from drowning."

My heart sank. My words had moved her to mercy, but not to abandon her plan to kill me. It looked like I would need magic after all, and I prayed that it worked before she sensed what I was doing.

I didn't have a spell that would force her to obey me and land safely on dry ground. My mind grasped for unconventional solutions. What about Asmodeus? I could summon him, pledge my fealty, and hope he would whisk me away.

No, I'd rather die than be so deeply indebted to a demon. I ran through other possibilities—milder magic that would be more difficult for her to detect. An itching spell? Nope, she'd just drop me to free her talons for scratching. Make her nauseous or have a bowel attack? No, birds love to poop when they fly.

I dimly remembered a spell that gives someone a fear of heights. This brought me hope until I realized she would simply drop me before descending to a lower altitude. The same result would occur if I conjured strong winds to force her down.

Why didn't I know a spell that enabled me to fly? Because only mages are powerful enough to do that. And no, they don't use broomsticks.

Fighting back panic, I forced my mind to keep it simple. And then it came to me. I remembered the most popular spell in witchcraft, practiced by amateurs, kitchen witches, wizards, and everyone in between. A spell conjured through potions, amulets, or pure elemental magic.

A love spell.

If Zora were heterosexual, my magic couldn't make her feel romantic love toward me, but it could make her love me like a sister. It was worth a try, and for someone as experienced as I, it was easy. I cast the spell.

"What are you doing?" Zora demanded. "I sense magic."

"Nothing. I'm just thinking about how well the Cryptids Society will take care of you. We want to keep you safe. I want to keep you safe."

Zora's flapping wings missed a beat. "You do?"

"Whether you're guilty, or innocent as you claim, we'll protect you from the flawed human justice system. We only want to study you. You're the first harpy I've ever met."

"You're so sweet. Why are you being nice to me? Are you doing it just to save your life?"

"I don't want to die. But I also don't want you to enter the human justice system and be executed or spend the rest of your life in prison." I was sincere about that. I believed Zora had been manipulated by Levings and treated poorly. She deserved only the most minor of punishments from the Society and not to face human jails at all.

"Why are you so sure they'll convict me? I told you I'm innocent."

Of course she'd say she was innocent. I didn't believe she was. But I had to get on her good side and hope my simple love spell was kicking in. My life depended on it.

"I believe you're innocent," I said. "But I can't guarantee the police will. Please trust me. Return home and meet with the Friends of Cryptids Society."

She didn't answer, so I asked, "Did Dr. Levings know you're a harpy?"

"No. No one knows."

"I'm honored that I know the real you."

She was silent. But a moment later, she banked smoothly to the left and flew back toward land.

"I do trust you," she said with genuine affection in her voice. It both warmed my heart and stung me with guilt for having swayed her with magic this way. Yes, she had intended to kill me, but manipulating her emotions seemed worse than fighting back with brute force.

When we returned to Zora's apartment complex, she placed me on the ground in a distant, empty part of the parking lot where there were no cars. I almost collapsed after the trauma I'd been through. Then Zora landed nearby, quickly transforming from harpy to human.

The Society's unmarked white van pulled up. Frankie was at the wheel. Mrs. Lupis and Mr. Lopez got out, clearly relieved to see Zora and me.

"Funny how I knew you'd still be here," I said.

"Your boyfriend didn't wait for you," said Mr. Lopez. "He drove west, looking at the sky, as if he believed he could rescue you."

"He's not my boyfriend. Mrs. Lupis and Mr. Lopez, allow me to introduce Zora. I promised her that the Society would keep her safe and treat her fairly, especially after she revealed that she's a mythological creature."

"It is a pleasure to meet you, Zora," said Mrs. Lupis. "I look forward to getting to know you. I've always wanted to study a harpy. However, first you must answer some questions about the death worms and how they came to kill six humans."

Two individuals exited the van, and I caught my breath. They wore gray suits and ties like the ones my handlers wore, but these creatures did not resemble humans. They were short and squat. Their large, round heads had no hair other than that which covered their chins beneath two large tusks that curved from their mouths to their noses.

"Come with us, please," the larger one said with a lisp.

Zora's eyes were wide with fear. She didn't move.

"Do not worry," Mrs. Lupis said. "You will be treated fairly."

I glanced at Mr. Lopez, and he nodded to me. But I felt uneasy. The Society's justice department now seemed even more sinister to me. I told myself I shouldn't allow the agents' scary appearances to influence my thinking, but now I worried about what would become of Zora.

And I had promised her she'd be safe.

"We're going with Zora to the Sanctuary now," Mrs. Lupis told me. "You can drive yourself home."

I watched the van leave with dread. And then I remembered Matt had taken the car. Long ago, I had given him my second key fob in case I lost mine or, more likely, had a supernatural disaster and needed to be rescued. It didn't mean he was my boyfriend, though.

I returned to Zora's apartment and fished my phone out from under the sofa.

"Are you safe?" Matt gushed when he answered my call.

"Yes. I'm at Zora's apartment. The Society just took her away for questioning."

"You didn't get dropped into the Gulf! Why don't you sound happy?"

"I was so certain that Zora was the killer. Now, I'm having second thoughts."

"The Society should be able to determine that."

"I'm having second thoughts about them, too."

Matt returned with my car and picked me up, eventually getting onto Alligator Alley for yet another drive back across the state. We didn't talk much until we reached Jellyfish Beach.

"I want to dig a little deeper into Zora," I said. "I want to make sure she's the real perpetrator."

Matt reached his bungalow and said goodnight. I drove my car home. But before I reached my street, an old four-door sedan coming toward me suddenly pulled into my lane and blocked me. Three men got out and surrounded my car. I recognized their leader.

It was Tim Tissy, who called himself Lord Arseton. These goons worked for Ruth, and they were here to turn my life upside down.

CHAPTER 23
SAINT RUTHLESS

"You've missed the last two coven meetings," Ruth said to me sternly from a throne at the end of the room, surrounded by massive black candles. She wore a purple robe with a hood that kept her face in shadow.

I stood in the middle of her living room, surrounded by coven members who sat on the floor cleared of furniture. Lord Arseton and his crew members who had abducted me, and several senior witches of the coven, all wore street clothes because this was an administrative meeting, not a black-magic ceremony.

"Even worse than your non-attendance," Ruth continued, "you haven't paid your dues for this month."

"Dues?" I retorted. "You mean protection money."

"If you don't like the term 'dues,' you can call it a tribute to my power and greatness."

I couldn't believe this woman was my birth mother. Fortunately, I had been adopted by a normal, loving family. I was strange enough as it was; if Ruth had raised me, I would have been a total freak.

"I've been busy and preoccupied," I said in as reasonable a tone as I could muster. "There's an invasive species running loose in Jellyfish Beach killing people."

"How delightful! Don't you just love this little city?"

"If you want me to attend coven meetings and pay dues, you must break the spell that binds me to Asmodeus."

Ruth cackled. "Why would I do that? He's my leverage to get you to obey. And if you don't obey, he will kill you. Which brings me back to the purpose of this meeting. I'm going to have him kill you today if you don't pay up."

"He's too powerful a demon to be your goon and debt collector, Ruth."

"Saint Ruthless."

"Sorry, Saint Ruthless. Asmodeus wants to use me to gain power in this world." I added, "He wants me to worship *him*, not you."

Ruth jerked forward on her throne, causing her hood to slip backward, revealing her enraged expression. "Sorcerers employ demons to serve *them*, not the other way around!"

"You need to remind Asmodeus of that and unbind me from him. If he subjugates me, I won't be able to worship you anymore."

"That is unacceptable!"

"If you want me to be a dutiful member of your coven, you must unbind me from the demon. Nothing else you say or do to me will make a difference if I'm stuck under the influence of Asmodeus."

"Very well," Ruth said in a sullen tone. "Pay this month's dues now, and I will do as you ask."

"Now? I don't have that much cash on me."

"I take credit cards." She clapped her hands. "Federico! Bring me the card reader."

Her rotund, middle-aged servant, clad in his red leotard, burst from the kitchen and waddled into the room, carrying the device. I reluctantly paid with my card.

"Bring me the brazier," she told him.

He disappeared into another room and returned with a shallow metal pan with short legs, which he placed on the floor in front of me. It reeked of burnt incense—rancid-smelling stuff. Squatting on his chubby, hairy legs, Federico lit the incense. The smoke swirled around me, the smell of it making me sick to my stomach. Federico hurried back to the kitchen, turning off the room's overhead lights before he disappeared.

The coven members knelt in a circle around the room, their heads bowed. Ruth stood and spread her arms wide in the oversized sleeves of her robe. Her first words came out as a croak, so she cleared her throat and tried again.

"Mighty Asmodeus, I summon you to earth under my authority as the mightiest sorcerer in the land."

She switched to a jumble of Latin and Hebrew. I didn't know what she was saying, but it sounded like it would convince a demon.

The skin on my arms and scalp tingled as magic spread throughout the room. Flames taller than me shot upward from the smoldering incense before subsiding.

"Asmodeus, Prince of Hell, I request that you appear before

me in the material world! By the power of my magic, I command you!"

The temperature in the room dropped at least twenty degrees, and I shivered. The people sitting in a circle around us gasped, and then I saw it: a hulking dark figure standing behind Ruth's throne, six eyes from three heads glowing red like the incense.

"Asmodeus, I hereby sever the bond that attaches you to this witch before me, Missy Mindle. Henceforth, you shall have no influence over her, and she shall have none over you. You are now free to return to your fiery realm."

"Sorry," said the deep voice emanating from the human head. "No can do."

Ruth sputtered. "Of course, you must obey me."

"I enjoy being bonded to this human. Her magic is powerful, and she has a lot of potential."

"She is *my* servant and is bonded only to *me*. Obey me, demon, and sever the bond."

"Listen, babe, I've been around since Creation, and I won't be pushed around by an old hag who chain-smokes cheap cigarettes. I'll decide if and when I'm finished with this human."

"But you must obey me!" Ruth's voice had lost its previous confidence. "My magic summoned you, so you must obey me."

"I came here because I wanted to. And you, witch," his red eyes bored into me, "you will obey *me*. I will pay another visit to you when you least expect it, and you will agree to worship me."

The dark figure and glowing eyes disappeared just as flames shot up from the brazier again. This time, the flames were larger and taller, hitting the ceiling and catching it on fire.

Two different smoke detectors in the apartment began shrieking, and the emergency sprinklers went off, drenching me and everyone else.

"Federico! Get the fire extinguisher!" Ruth screamed.

As the people in the room scurried about like beetles from beneath an overturned rock, I tiptoed through the smoke and raining water before slipping out the front door.

Great, I thought as I left the building. *I'm still bonded to Asmodeus, plus I had to pay my dues after all.* After my grumbling, I remembered something: Dr. Hooey had mentioned the Society studied demons in addition to monsters. I was skeptical that they could help me, but I felt like I had no choice but to ask.

"DEMONS? Yeah, we study them from time to time," Mr. Lopez said. "It's difficult to gather data about them. Usually, we encounter them when they're possessing a creature, and all we see is their personality and intellect. It's rare that you come across a demon in its physical manifestation. Very rare. And it takes incredible luck to catch a demon in its natural form and keep it that way."

Mrs. Lupis gave him a shut-your-pie-hole look. "Why do you ask, Missy?"

"Well, Dr. Hooey mentioned the study of demons, and I was wondering if the Society could help me. You see, I have a demon problem." I told them the story of Asmodeus and me.

"Asmodeus? He's bad news," Mr. Lopez said.

"You need to break the bond," his partner added. "If not, you could be bonded to him for the rest of your life. Even after you die."

"Oh, my. Can you help me?"

"We must help her," Mr. Lopez said.

"Okay, we will. We'll introduce her to Dr. Davis, our demonologist. She'll know what to do."

Once again, I drove my handlers to the national wildlife preserve and the alternate universe that was hidden inside it, where the Cryptid Sanctuary existed. I followed them through the extensive building where the most dangerous creatures and entities were held, keeping them out of the real world to prevent death and destruction and for scientific study.

I'd been inside this building once before. It was where Rachel, the murderous sprite, lived. The place gave me the creeps.

Dr. Davis was a youngish Asian American who appeared too good-natured to devote her days to demons. I told my story about Asmodeus again, this time with more details. Dr. Davis nodded politely throughout my tale, not acting surprised by any of it.

"Why, since the beginning of time, have humans summoned demons?" she asked rhetorically. "It always ends badly. And we already have too many demons visiting the world on their own. We don't need to summon more."

"Agreed," said Mrs. Lupis.

"If magic or religion didn't work on this demon, there's only one thing he'll respect: a more powerful demon."

"Oh, my," I said, not liking where this was going.

"Demons are very obsessed with their hierarchies," Dr. Davis continued.

"Asmodeus is as high ranked as they come," I said.

"No, there's one higher rung on the ladder. Lucifer."

"Well, duh."

"Lucifer is here."

It took a moment for that to sink in. "You mean *here?* Like, in the Sanctuary?"

"We captured him in his physical form and have kept him here under the highest security. Mind you, Lucifer, or Satan if you prefer, still exerts his negative influence on humans. But physically, he's stuck here. And we believe that's a good thing."

"So, Lucifer will convince Asmodeus to break the bond and go home to hell?"

"He'll order him to. And Asmodeus must obey. The tricky part will be convincing Lucifer to intercede on your behalf. I suppose bribery will work. Come with me and meet him."

Mrs. Lupis and Mr. Lopez declined to accompany us; they had no desire to meet the paragon of evil. I felt the same but had no choice if I wanted to rid myself of my demon.

I followed Dr. Davis along several windowless corridors, through three different security doors with armed guards who were human or at least were in human form.

"We employ an overabundance of security here," Dr. Davis explained. "Lucifer isn't very strong in his material form, but the fear is he'll recruit cryptids or humans to help him escape."

"How do you keep him in material form?"

"That's a trade secret," she replied with a wry smile.

At last, we arrived at a cell made of unbreakable glass. It looked like a luxurious studio apartment. Lucifer sat in a contemporary-style easy chair, typing on a laptop. He was dressed in a blue suit with a red tie like a politician, and he had a pleasant, bland face like a television news anchorman, topped by a thick head of moussed black hair. He ignored us as he typed away.

"He's in human form?" I asked, incredulous. "I expected a hideous chimera made of different creatures, like Asmodeus."

"When on earth physically, Lucifer takes on the form of the evilest creature that exists on this planet."

A human. It took me a moment to digest that.

"What is he doing on the laptop?" I asked.

"He spends all his time on social media, spinning conspiracy theories and stoking division, distrust, and unrest. After all, he's the paragon of evil."

"Why do you allow him to do that?"

"It's a compromise of sorts. Lucifer will bring evil to the world no matter what we do. By confining him to the internet, we limit the scope of the evil. Somewhat. We can always shut down his connection if things get out of hand, before he creates an apocalypse."

"I hope you closely monitor what he's posting."

"We do." She grimaced. "It's terribly traumatic, really."

She knocked on the glass, and Lucifer looked up. He took a keen interest in me, piercing me with icy blue eyes while wearing a flirtatious grin.

"Don't fall for his tricks," Dr. Davis said to me. She pressed the button of an intercom mounted on the safety glass. "Lucifer, how are you today?"

"As miserable as always during my illegal confinement. Who is this stunning creature before me?"

"Her name is Missy Mindle."

I gave him a little wave. He blew me a kiss that excited me and curdled my stomach at the same time.

"Enchanted," he said. "May I ask why you're here? You're a witch, aren't you?"

"I am," I said into the intercom.

"I hope you're not here to request help with black magic."

"Oh, no. Not at all."

"I know you have a request. Humans want nothing from me, other than preachers who want to destroy me, or conniving individuals who want my assistance in gaming the system."

I glanced at Dr. Davis. She shook her head and removed her finger from the intercom button. "You're the only visitor he's had in months."

I pressed the button. "I'm not conniving. I'm beset by a demon."

"Oh?" He seemed interested.

"Asmodeus." I recounted the story.

"I take it you want me to intervene."

"Yes, sir, please." I wasn't sure if one should call the Prince of Darkness "sir," or something more extravagant, but it was what came out of my mouth.

"What's in it for me?"

"We'll extend your internet privileges one hour a day," Dr. Davis said.

I cringed. An hour more of poison poured into the bloodstream of society, creating hatred and maybe even causing people to get hurt. But I was desperate.

"You want me to order Asmodeus to break his bond with you?" Lucifer asked.

"Yes, sir. And to leave me alone forever."

"I never liked that demon," he said, closing his laptop. "He's always wanted to usurp power from me. So, I agree to help you. I'll send him my command today."

"Thank you, sir."

"In return for future favors."

Dr. Davis looked at me sternly and shook her head.

"I can't promise anything," I said.

"Your birth mother, the sorceress, has profited much from evil, from the help of my army of demons. Yet she is an unbearable narcissist. She even calls herself a saint. I would like you to knock her down a peg or two."

"I would like nothing more than to do that. But I can't make a deal with the Devil."

He laughed. It wasn't the deep, diabolical laugh you'd expect from Lucifer. It was a high-pitched giggle that was very unflattering. "I'll keep an eye on you and hope you put her in her place."

"We're in agreement about Asmodeus?" Dr. Davis asked him.

He nodded. "An hour more each night on the internet and I'll send the three-headed chump packing right away. How splendid that the Friends of Cryptids Society is unafraid of making a deal with me!"

His annoying giggling continued until Dr. Davis removed her finger from the intercom button, and we left the cell behind.

"I didn't commit to doing what he wanted, did I?" I asked.

"No," Dr. Davis said. "However, he left you with his power

of suggestion, which is how he enacts much of his evil influence in the world."

I wasn't very pleased to hear that, but the fact was I had wanted to bring Ruth down for years, so I didn't care what Lucifer wanted.

"Let's go to the employee cafeteria," Dr. Davis said. "Mrs. Lupis and Mr. Lopez are waiting for you there."

The cafeteria looked like one you'd find in a corporate headquarters or hospital, with a salad bar and decorative ferns. We ate at a table with my handlers, and I munched on a chicken salad sandwich that was surprisingly good for one made in an alternate universe. I thanked them all for a mission accomplished.

"How are you guys?" It was Dr. Hooey, who had appeared beside our table, smiling pleasantly. He held a plastic tray with the remains of his lunch.

We each said hello.

"I wanted to thank you, Ms. Mindle, for your help in tackling our worm problem," he said. "I heard you successfully summoned one with the pungi, correct?"

"Yes. With terrible music."

"No worries. Now we have proof the pungi can summon them. So far, it's the only effective way we know of. We have the person who planted the worms in the victims' homes in custody?"

"She's being interrogated as we speak," Mrs. Lupis said.

"Fabulous! All that remains is to capture and destroy the remaining worms in the wild, and all will be good."

"I thought you loved the death worm passionately," I said. "Why do you want to destroy them?"

"They are a deadly invasive species. The Society has a small collection of the worms now, and that's all I need for my research. What's important to me is to keep the species hidden from human society. Humans would only exploit and debase these magnificent creatures."

Everyone at the table nodded.

"Here at the Society, we are the only ones in the world who understand, respect, and properly manage the cryptid populations," Dr. Hooey said. "Unlike human cryptozoologists, who study creatures for personal fame and fortune. To sell books about them. What a mockery! We *must* keep the worms hidden from humans and known to them only as a legend." He glanced at his watch. "I have a dissection to complete. Please keep me updated on your progress rounding up the worms."

He walked away in a great hurry. There was something off about the guy, even considering he wasn't human.

We continued eating in silence until I asked, "Will Zora be freed if she's found innocent?"

"I don't believe she'll be found innocent," Mrs. Lupis said.

"Since I'm here, can I visit her?"

"No," my handlers replied at the exact same time.

Why did I have such an uneasy feeling?

CHAPTER 24
A VEXING HEXING

I called Matt as soon as I arrived home.

"How was your trip to the Sanctuary?" he asked.

"Interesting. I met Lucifer."

"Lucifer, who?"

"Lucifer. Satan. The Devil. The original Fallen Angel."

"You mean he actually exists outside of theological literature?"

"Matt, your truck was snatched off the highway by a thirty-foot-tall demon, but you can't believe that the Devil exists?"

"Okay, if you put it that way. What was he doing at the Sanctuary?"

"He's imprisoned there in human form. Somehow, they've kept him stuck as a physical entity, so they've got him locked up."

"Then why is there still evil in the world?"

"His evil cannot be contained. Also, he spends his time spreading evil throughout social media."

"Ah, I think I've come across his posts." Matt chuckled. "Like, everywhere."

"I'm sure you have. The scientist studying him convinced him to help me. Lucifer promised to order Asmodeus to break his bonds with me and stay away."

"Wow, the Devil did a good deed."

"We'll see if he did or not. Listen, I'm still worried about Zora. Did we falsely accuse her?"

"The Society should figure out if she's guilty. Did you see her there?"

"No. They wouldn't allow me to. And there's something else." I glanced around my kitchen, paranoid that someone might be spying on me. "Dr. Hooey, the ickologist."

"Obviously, I've never met him."

"He's a strange character, not only because of his specialty. He's completely obsessed with Mongolian Death Worms."

"So were Milo and Dr. Levings."

"They're like casual hobbyists compared to Dr. Hooey. He's extremely adamant that the worms must not be discovered by the public. He wants us to remove all of them and doesn't care if they're destroyed because they're an invasive species. But most of all, he wants to keep them secret."

"I guess the Cryptids Society wants to be the sole proprietor of cryptids."

I agreed. "Yeah, something like that. And he had utter contempt for the two cryptozoologists. He said they searched only for the worm out of a desire to be famous. He mentioned their unpublished books."

"How would he know about the books?"

"I have no idea. But it made me suspicious. If we believe Dr.

Levings killed Milo to prevent him from publishing, we have to consider whether Dr. Hooey would do the same thing."

Matt snorted. "Come on, be serious."

"I am. He believed worms could be summoned by someone playing the pungi. What if he had proof his theory was correct because he successfully summoned a worm? And he could have brought it back to the United States."

"Not necessarily. He could have learned about the pungi from native Mongolians."

"The pungi I have is from India. In all the reading I've done, I've never seen a mention of Mongolians using pungis to summon worms. And he wouldn't have told me to use a pungi if he wasn't confident it would work."

Matt was silent.

"Are you still there?" I asked.

"Yes. It's just a lot to take in. Are you going to mention anything about Hooey to your handlers?"

"I should. I really should. They probably won't take me seriously, but it's my obligation to find the truth."

"Maybe it's too risky to accuse someone from the Society."

"It would be too cowardly for me to stay silent."

We hung up, and I texted Mrs. Lupis. *We need to talk. I have questions about Dr. Hooey.*

I waited for an answer, and my doorbell rang. I sighed, shook my head, and opened the front door.

"And you just happened to be in the neighborhood?" I asked my handlers who were standing on the porch.

"As a matter of fact, we were," Mr. Lopez replied.

"What are your questions about Dr. Hooey?" Mrs. Lupis asked.

I paused. Caution was required. "Has he ever visited Mongolia?"

"I would assume so. He's an expert on the death worm."

"I'm wondering if he might have captured a worm there. The worm that killed Claire Fusseldink and started this saga."

"Are you accusing him of *murder*?" Mrs. Lupis was offended. "He's the world's most renowned ickologist,"

"He's the world's *only* ickologist," said Mr. Lopez. "Which makes it rather easy to be the most renowned one."

"I refuse to entertain the possibility that he committed murder."

"Same here."

"Why are you so blindly supportive of him?" I asked. "Because he works for the Society?"

They nodded.

I sensed there was more to the story, though. "Or is it because he's the same species as you?"

They looked as if I'd thrown water in their faces.

Mrs. Lupis said, "That's none of your concern."

"Completely irrelevant," said Mr. Lopez.

"I apologize for asking," I said. "It's only because you've both already admitted that you once lived in the cryptid dorms at the Sanctuary. And Dr. Hooey said that you and he came from the Land of Faerie."

"He said that?" Mr. Lopez asked.

"He talks too much," his partner added.

"I would have thought that after all this time we've worked together, you'd want to be open and honest with me about your backgrounds."

"We never thought it was relevant," Mr. Lopez said.

"It would be helpful to me," I said. "Learning about the secret creatures of our world is my life now, thanks to you guys. You can't blame me for my desire to know."

"If you insist," said Mrs. Lupis. "It is true that we were born in the Land of Faerie."

The Land of Faerie was not a geographical location on Earth or any planet. Like the Sanctuary, it existed in an alternate universe beside ours.

"Are you Fae?" There, I did it. I asked what I'd been suspecting.

Mrs. Lupis shook her head. "No, we're not Fae."

"I understand that other people besides the Fae live in the Land of Faerie," I said, hoping they would complete the thought.

"Yes," said Mr. Lopez, struggling with his admission. "We're pixies."

"Oh," I replied, somewhat surprised. "That's awesome."

"We're like the Fae," he continued, "but are more magical. And less warlike."

"And we can fly when we're in our natural forms," Mrs. Lupis said.

Their admission explained a lot to me. "Ah, so that's how you always end up at my doorstep seconds after I think about you. Thank you for finally sharing your secret with me. Is Dr. Hooey also a pixie?"

They nodded.

"Why is he so obsessed with the death worm?"

"He's obsessed with everything he studies," Mrs. Lupis said. "It's a characteristic of our species."

"But he takes it a little too far," said Mr. Lopez.

"Shouldn't we look into him as a suspect in the worm deaths?" I asked. "If only to rule him out?"

"Perhaps we will mention him to the justice agents," Mrs. Lupis said.

"They're orcs, by the way," her partner added. "But they don't come from the Land of Faerie. They're from Wisconsin."

After they left, I saw Tony through the window munching on a neighbor's orchids. Normally, I would scold him, but I felt sorry for his suffering under Ruth's muting spell.

I called her, and surprisingly for someone who usually slept off hangovers for most of the day, she answered.

"It's time to reset our relationship," I said.

"Good luck with that." Her voice was a croak.

"I believe I've gotten Asmodeus off my back. Now, I need you to break your hex on my familiar, and I'll return to learning black magic from you."

"You didn't break the bond with Asmodeus. If I couldn't do it, you sure as heck didn't."

"Lucifer commanded him to leave me alone."

"*Lucifer?* What have you been smoking, dearie?"

"The Cryptids Society has a special, um, arrangement with him. They convinced him to help me."

"That's pure bull-puckey."

"Lucifer told me he's aware of you and is not happy that you're calling yourself a saint. He wants you to show more respect for him and his demons."

Ruth was silent before snorting with derision. "Nonsense."

"Saint Ruthless, I can intercede with Lucifer for you and protect you from his wrath. All I ask is that you break the hex on my iguana."

"I will not, until you pay your dues and resume your training."

"I paid my dues the last time I saw you."

"You owe me a late fee!"

I ended the call. Pleading with her was a waste of time.

Ruth called me back. "How dare you hang up on me!"

"If you're not going to respect me, I won't respect you."

"I am the mighty Saint Ruthless! The most powerful sorceress in the world!"

"Oh, come on."

"The most powerful in America . . . okay, the most powerful in this part of Florida. You will respect me, or I will kill you!"

I ended the call again. She did not call back. I figured she was stewing with anger and plotting how she would kill me.

If I had truly gotten Asmodeus off my back, why couldn't I defeat Ruth in other ways? Why couldn't I break her muting spell myself so that Tony could speak again and serve me properly as my witch's familiar?

I had defeated Ruth's magic in the past. Though this hex was powerful, I could probably break it if I put my mind to it. It was time to prove to myself that my natural, elemental magic—white magic, if you will—could be more powerful than black magic.

Deep inside, I had been attracted by the allure of black magic, by the promises that it was more powerful than what benevolent magicians could conjure. I had fooled myself by imagining I could use black magic for good.

I was wrong. Black magic was evil. It was powered by demons, blood, and death. It would never lead to anything good. In contrast, my spells were enabled by the magic gene I had been born with, powered by my internal energies and the energy I derived from the earth, air, water, fire, and the life spirit.

In short, my magic was natural. Ruth's was a perversion. It was time to put my hope in myself.

With Tony only being able to communicate using the Ouija board, he would be of little help in devising a spell to break Ruth's. So, I summoned Don Mateo. He didn't come. Impatient, I went into my bedroom and grabbed panties from my dresser, twirling them above my head.

"Don Mateo! I need you *now*," I shouted, sending the cats dashing under the bed.

The underwear was yanked from my fingers, and Don Mateo appeared before me, clutching the panties. "Oh, my apologies. Does this garment belong to you?"

I snatched it back. Ghosts, except for poltergeists, have little physical strength. "I need you to help me devise a spell to free Tony from his hex."

"I would be honored to help Antonio, M'lady, but you don't have the power to defeat black magic. Not your mother's."

"Don't call her my mother. And I believe we can figure out a way to do it. Our cleverness can overcome her power."

"I cannot say I'm clever, considering the fact that it was my reckless summoning of a demon that took my life."

"Buck up, my friend, and let's do this. What spells do you

know involving blood? From what I've seen, a great deal of Ruth's black magic uses blood offerings to demons and other evil entities. Perhaps there's something we can do with Tony's blood to negate the hex."

"Did Ruth use his blood when she hexed him?" Don Mateo asked.

"No. I don't believe she used any blood at all. That's why I believe using Tony's will make our spell stronger than hers."

"Surely, you do not intend to use black magic?"

"No." I was losing my patience. "I want to find an old spell, from back in the days when blood was often mixed into the ingredients of a magic potion. I'm talking about white magic, elemental magic. *Not* black magic. We can adapt the old spell to our needs."

"Thank you, M'lady. That was very helpful. Let's consult my grimoire."

Don Mateo was referring to the ancient spell book he used when he was a living wizard in Spain. When he fled to Colonial Florida to escape the Spanish Inquisition, he hand-wrote Native American spells in the back pages. The grimoire was one of my most valuable possessions.

I removed the grimoire from its hiding place beneath the cats' litter box, where no burglar would want to search, and placed it on my kitchen table. Don Mateo's ghostly hand flipped through the pages.

"Ah," he said, "here's a spell purporting to treat the deaf and the mute. Surely, it was ineffective, but it was the best they could do in the Middle Ages. I believe that with your power and expertise, and a few drops of Tony's blood, we can use its framework to create the spell you're envisioning."

I went into the garage to create a poultice as the spell instructed, while Don Mateo revised the Latin incantation. Thanks to working in a botanica, I was well stocked with the arcane ingredients required: everything from songbird feathers and dried cicadas to licorice and sage. I even had a small vial of ear hair plucked from aging men, who grew it in abundance. Yes, I really did. Tony's hearing was fine, but the spell's recipe called for it.

The only problem in making my recipe was getting the key ingredient: Tony's blood. I'd never seen an iguana's eyes bulge in horror like that before.

Iguanas can run surprisingly fast. Tony's little green legs, extending perpendicularly from his body, moved so quickly they were a blur. I chased him all over the house, but when he escaped through the open garage door window, I was forced to use my sleep spell on him. He lay on my lawn like the stunned iguanas that fall from trees during cold fronts. I brought him inside and extracted the blood painlessly before waking him up and placing him in the magic circle I had already drawn on my kitchen floor.

I spread the poultice all over his body, commanding him to remain still while I gathered my internal energies and then added energy from the element of earth. I activated the poultice with the magical energies and recited the incantation Don Mateo had revised. The spell was complete.

"Are we done yet?" The New-York accented voice, that had been absent from my life for so long, asked. "This junk you spread on me stinks like a freaking landfill!"

"Tony, you're back! Let me wash you off."

"It is wonderful to hear your voice again, Antonio," Don Mateo said before his apparition faded away.

"Let's test if your telepathy is working again," I said.

Don't let that evil woman hex me ever again, said Tony in my head.

I promise I won't.

THAT NIGHT, Matt and I were at the beach hunting death worms in the moonlight. Playing the pungi worked well to bring them to the surface, but we captured only three, which had surfaced one at a time.

"I'd thought there would be a bunch of them, like the time we were attacked out here," I said.

"Maybe it's because your pungi playing is so horrible," Matt snarked.

"I've improved. Admit it. I'm wondering if our problem is the high tide. Dr. Hooey had said the worms would have an aversion to saltwater."

After Frankie showed up in the white van to cart the worms away, I was truly thankful I had broken Tony's hex. Because the wards around my house went off, warning of an intruder.

And Tony's telepathic voice blared in my head: *Someone broke into the house and locked me in the garage. I don't know who it is or what they're doing, but you better get here fast!*

CHAPTER 25
HOME INTRUDER

Matt and I were exceedingly cautious when we arrived at my house. First, we made sure there were no unfamiliar cars parked nearby. Next, we examined the outside, just as we had when we caught Zora. No doors appeared to have been tampered with, so I unlocked the kitchen door in the rear of the house, and we entered quietly.

There was complete silence, save for the ticking of the antique clock in the living room. I cast a spell that heightened my senses and stood still for an unbearably long time, listening for any sound of an intruder, trying to catch a scent that didn't belong, and feeling for supernatural energy. There was nothing.

I checked on the cats. They were in my bedroom, standing on my bed, looking distressed. Surprisingly, they weren't hiding under the bed. Next, I checked Don Mateo's grimoire. It was still in its hiding place. Then, I went to check on Tony. Notice how I didn't check on my jewelry, checkbook, or hidden cash first? It was pretty telling what my priorities were.

"It took you forever to get here!" Tony whined when I unlocked and opened the door in the laundry room that led to the garage.

I shushed him.

"I don't need to be quiet. The intruder left long ago."

"What exactly did they do?"

"I'm not sure. I was sleeping on my perch in the garage when I heard the wards go off in my head. Before I could do anything, he locked the door to the house from the inside. Thanks to your closing the window, I couldn't get out that way."

"You said 'he.' How do you know it was a man?"

"Who says it was a man? My intuition told me it was a male, but I sensed he wasn't human. I heard him walk around the house briefly before he left through the kitchen door."

"Maybe it's time to get a guard dog," Matt said. "Tony's not much of a guard lizard."

"Watch your mouth, pencil neck!" Tony said in his most thuggish tone. He was a large iguana, but Matt was clearly not intimidated.

"I'm going to keep searching for anything missing," I said, going inside. Matt and Tony followed.

With my non-human family safe and sound, I took an inventory of my financial items. My hidden emergency cash and extra credit card were where I had hidden them. I went into the master bedroom to check on my jewelry and the box of tax information in the closet.

Why were Bubba and Brenda still standing on the bed as if escaping from rising floodwaters?

I soon got my answer. I caught a whiff of cinnamon, along

with an odd, acrid smell. And from under the bed came the rhythmic sliding of something on the carpet.

"Matt!" I shouted. "Watch out for worms!"

Stepping away from the bed, I prepared the freezing spell. The bedskirt rustled, and a reddish-brown head poked through. I jumped into the closet, barely avoiding the stream of amber venom that shot across the room and splattered against the wall.

Was it I who screamed? No, it couldn't have been me, I thought, my throat raw from screaming.

I threw a shoe at the worm, hitting the bed frame just above the creature. It withdrew from sight. I returned my focus to gathering my energies and casting the spell, and when the worm ventured forth from the bed again, I blasted it with Arctic air.

And then another worm slithered out, heading toward my closet refuge, sidewinding as well as inching up its rear section. It reared its head and opened its hideous maw. I shot it with magic before it could spit venom at me.

Two worms, frozen. Were there any more in the house?

In the kitchen, Matt shrieked like a little girl. Okay, there was at least a third worm.

I ran to the kitchen where Matt crouched on top of the island. A death worm slithered around the base of a bar stool, its front section raised vertically like a cobra, trying to find an angle for sending venom at Matt. It turned to face me, and I zapped it with my cold spell. It fell over sideways and lay on the floor like a taxidermy specimen in a museum.

"I got him," I said.

The cabinet beneath the sink burst open. Make that four

worms in my house. A bottle of dish detergent and a can of furniture polish fell from the cabinet as the worm emerged and raised its head, aiming at Matt on the island. I froze the worm just in time.

"This is crazy!" Matt exclaimed. "How many worms did the intruder bring to your house?"

"Four. I froze two in my bedroom."

"Can you imagine going to sleep and waking up with worms in your face?"

I shuddered at the thought. "*Four* worms. Can you believe it? The intruder didn't want any chance that I'd escape."

"Five worms," Tony said from the top of the refrigerator. I hadn't noticed him before. "The spice cabinet."

Sure enough, the doors of the cabinet next to the fridge opened as a worm slithered out and dropped onto the counter. I cringed at the thought of the nasty thing touching my food prep area.

"Freeze him!" Matt urged.

"I'm trying. My energies are low from all the magic I've expended. I need to replenish them."

Tony muttered a particularly foul curse that sounded even worse in his New York accent. He jumped from the fridge onto the top shelf of the open cabinet, opening a box of kosher salt and pushing it over, dumping its contents upon the worm below him.

The worm convulsed, flipping about on the counter like an earthworm on a street curb. It made a strange keening sound and stopped moving. It looked dead, having shrunk to half its previous size.

"Amazing," Matt said. "You can kill them with salt like

slugs. You wouldn't think so, because their skin is tougher than a slug's. Maybe it has something to do with glands they used to retain water in a desert environment."

"Enough of your scientific hypotheses," I said. "Let's make sure there aren't any more worms in my house."

Matt, Tony, and I searched the house. Tony struggled to open drawers, but he could only open cabinets that were within reach. We looked everywhere: in every room, every closet, every storage space, beneath and behind every piece of furniture. I found several missing cat toys under the furniture and an earring I had lost months ago. So, there was a bright side.

The garage presented the most challenging search because it was so filled with junk. The one-car space had no room for a car. It served as my workshop for mixing dangerous and noxious potions and, of course, was where I stored lawn tools and supplies. Since my home lacked a basement, as did most throughout Florida, my garage was filled with lots of crap I should have gotten rid of but hadn't.

Tony had been in here when the intruder entered the house, so we knew no worms had been deposited here. Yet there was the chance that one or more worms slipped in here afterwards. It was nerve-racking searching through the boxes and behind bags of mulch in the poorly lit space.

A scratching sound came from behind me. I jumped, Matt gasped, and Tony cursed.

It was only a mouse. Normally, I would be upset to find a mouse in my garage. Tonight, I was relieved by the furry little creature.

When we were confident that the garage was free of worms, I grabbed a beer for Matt from the extra fridge out here, and we went inside. Matt sipped his beer on the living room couch while I poured myself a glass of wine and gave Tony a fresh tomato.

When I walked into the living room, I flicked a wall switch that turned on two lamps. My heart froze.

Inside the illuminated lampshade near Matt was a dark shape that moved. A worm dropped onto the end table. Matt tried to move away, but a jet of venom shot from the worm and hit him in the face. He screamed and clawed at his face, then slid to the floor, where he lay unmoving. He gasped for air. The worm slithered toward him across the couch, its mouth open and teeth dripping venom.

"Omigod, omigod, omigod!" I moaned with anguish as I reactivated my magic and froze the worm before it could take a bite of Matt. Rushing to him, I pushed away the coffee table and checked his pulse. His heart beat weakly, and he struggled to breathe. Despite the goofy smile of euphoria on his face, he was losing the battle to live.

I called 911 and begged them to hurry, but Matt was fading fast. I had to muster both my nursing skills and magic to save him. Would black magic have come in handy now? Maybe, but I pushed the thought from my mind.

I placed sofa cushions under his torso and legs to keep his head lower than his body, hoping that would slow the spread of venom through his bloodstream. His face was covered with yellow burns, and his breathing was growing shallower. I was ready to intervene with CPR, but there was little I could do medically. He needed antivenom, but the kind the paramedics would have—for treating bites from the most common venomous snakes, spiders, and scorpions—might not work with death-worm venom.

My magic might be Matt's only hope. But I couldn't think of any spells that would save him.

In the history of magic, you could find a spell for just about anything. A good many simply didn't work; experienced witches have spent lifetimes using trial and error to discard the useless ones and memorize the good ones. When it came to healing, most spells were lousy until medical science came along and doctors performed their own version of magic.

Still, there were a few that have worked since the Dark Ages. Finally, I remembered an antidote spell written in the era when assassins preferred poison as their weapon of choice. It cleansed the blood of such poisons as hemlock and arsenic. But would it work on death-worm venom?

Before I cast it, I bent over and kissed Matt on his cheek where it was still damp from the venom. The burning on my lips was unbearable. I licked them with my tongue to better absorb the venom into my system, not enough to kill me but just enough to influence my spell.

My heart skipped a beat and slowed. I felt dizzy. But I forced myself into a semi-trance state through sheer determination. I gathered my energies and enhanced their power by gripping the Red Dragon talisman in my pocket. Finally, I placed my left hand on Matt's head and my right on his chest.

The incantation was short and simple: all about purifying the patient's blood, heart, and soul. I sent the magic into Matt, waited for it to flood his body and absorb the death energy, then I drew it back out of him, being careful that it flowed not into me but into the earth.

I waited. Matt remained unconscious, but he continued to breathe steadily, and his heart rate picked up slightly. There was nothing else I could do but pray.

When the paramedics arrived, I pushed the cold-stunned worm under the sofa before they could see it. One of them remarked she had worked on the jogger on the beach with the same symptoms as Matt. She didn't mention the obvious fact that her patient had died.

After she had injected the antivenom and hooked Matt to an IV, she and her partner placed him on a gurney and rolled him to the ambulance. I insisted on riding with them to the hospital. Along the way, I texted Mrs. Lupis and told her there were six worms in my house that needed to be picked up.

When we pulled into the ER bay, Matt suddenly opened his eyes.

"Whoa, dude, what happened to me?"

"Don't you remember you got sprayed by a death worm?" I didn't care that the paramedic in the back with us heard what I'd said.

"What saved me?"

"Antivenom," I said and exchanged a smile with the paramedic.

The truth was that the antivenom would be critical for his recovery. But I knew that he would have been dead before the paramedics arrived had it not been for my antidote spell.

HOURS LATER, when I knew Matt would be okay, I took a rideshare home from the hospital. Tony was waiting for me on the table in the foyer. I told him that Matt was okay.

"That was a powerful spell you used," he said.

I only nodded and didn't share my emotions about saving Matt's life. "I don't see any frozen worms. The Society picked them up?"

"Yeah. A couple of weirdos in white overalls. They were in human form, but I don't know what they were. You know, I was thinking about the funky gourd flute you used to hunt worms at the beach. Can I examine it?"

I took it from the closet and placed it on the table in front of him. "Here. It's called a pungi."

He touched the instrument with his claws and sniffed it. "It has magic in it."

"It does? I hadn't noticed. I wonder if it helps attract the worms."

"No, it's not that kind of magic. And the reason you hadn't noticed it was because it was meant to go unnoticed. It's a type of ward—a surveillance ward."

My mind refused to grasp the implications.

"The guy who gave you the pungi was surveilling you," Tony said. "He could listen to your conversations. And he knew when you took the pungi to the beach. It could have been him who broke into your house and dropped off the worms when he knew you weren't here."

"Oh, my. Dr. Hooey heard Matt and me debating whether

he was the killer. And he tried to eliminate me like he'd done with everyone else."

I called Mrs. Lupis and told her what I'd discovered. "Don't let Dr. Hooey escape. He needs to be interrogated."

"Are you absolutely certain?"

"Yes. Don't let him get away. And bring me to the Sanctuary as soon as possible."

CHAPTER 26

CLOSING THE CAN OF WORMS

I had expected Mrs. Lupis and Mr. Lopez to show up at my front door and ride with me to the Sanctuary. While I knew the location of the secret road that led there, I couldn't make it there on my own. I had to be accompanied by a full-time employee of the Society in order to transition into the alternate universe.

Instead of my handlers, Frankie showed up at my house in his white van. I climbed into the passenger seat and hung on while he drove at high speed through Jellyfish Beach to the national wildlife preserve and the entrance to the Sanctuary.

"Mrs. Lupis and Mr. Lopez couldn't make it?" I asked the goblin during the drive.

"They are in high-level meetings with the administration," he said in his odd accent. "Regarding the situation."

The situation being that one of their most senior scientists was guilty of murder by death worm. Frankie clearly didn't want to make small talk, so I remained silent for the rest of the drive.

Once we'd parked in the Sanctuary, Frankie led me to the same building that housed Lucifer and other high-risk detainees. He dropped me off outside a conference room and left as quickly as he could.

I went into the room. My handlers sat at a rectangular table and barely acknowledged me. Mrs. Lupis sulked; Mr. Lopez stewed with anger. I couldn't tell if they were unhappy with me or with the situation in general. A woman with silver hair and a long green dress entered the room, and my handlers straightened in their chairs.

"I am Margaret Bullfinch, director of the Sanctuary and Senior VP of the Friends of Cryptids Society of the Americas." She offered me her hand.

I shook it. "Missy Mindle. Pleased to meet you."

"Thank you for your excellent sleuthing," she said. "The culpability of an esteemed member of our team has been painful for our organization, but we must do what is necessary to achieve justice."

"Has Dr. Hooey admitted anything?"

"The interrogations are beginning to bear fruit. Dr. Hooey appears eager to brag about his deadly accomplishments."

She pressed a button on the table, and a decorative wall panel slid to the side to uncover a two-way mirror showing an adjoining room. The two orcs I had encountered before sat on one side of a small table, across from Dr. Hooey. The setup looked just like the interrogation rooms you see in police shows. Except for the orcs, of course.

The orcs frowned beneath their tusks as their species always does, while Dr. Hooey was smiling and animated. His hairpiece was slightly askew.

"As I've already told you, I did not intend for Mrs. Fusseldink to die," the ickologist said. "I'd heard rumors that Milo was not dead in the Gobi Desert, but was hiding somewhere, and I expected him to return to the US soon. So, I placed the worm in his dresser to ambush him. It was fitting that he should die from the creature he exploited."

"How did you avoid being recorded by the security cameras when you broke into the Fusseldink house?" the larger orc asked.

Dr. Hooey snorted arrogantly. "I'm a pixie. My magic cloaks me from human technology. You orcs can't imagine how convenient it is."

"You just left the worm in his dresser?"

"Death worms can live for weeks without nourishment, and I was certain Milo would return soon and open the drawer. It was only later that I discovered he was living in an apartment."

"How did you discover that?" asked the smaller orc.

"I followed Dr. Levings's assistant. She was spying on Milo."

The orcs scribbled on writing pads. The smaller orc asked, "Tell us again how you caught the worm that killed Mrs. Fusseldink. How did you find one when no other explorers could?"

"A pungi." Dr. Hooey beamed with pride. "A reed flute made from a gourd in India. They use them to charm cobras, and I had a theory that the right pitch and the right vibrations would summon death worms to the surface. I was correct."

"The original worm escaped to the beach. Did you recapture it to kill Milo Fusseldink?"

"No. That would have been nearly impossible. But, you see, the worms are capable of parthenogenesis—reproduction without mating. The original worm produced offspring, which grow extremely rapidly. With my pungi, I captured several from the beach."

"And the worm that killed Dr. Levings?"

Dr. Hooey smirked. "Pride cometh before the fall. Dr. Levings apparently caught one of the offspring on the beach himself and displayed it in a terrarium in his home. I freed it, so he would be killed by his own worm."

The ickologist crossed his arms and stared smugly at the justice agents.

The larger orc spoke. "You wouldn't answer us before when we asked you the simple question: why did you kill the cryptozoologists?"

"They were pseudoscientific hacks who had no interest in the death worms, other than to boost their careers and make money. Both were planning to publish books about the species. Milo had molted skin to prove his case. After Levings acquired a living specimen, his book would have been even more dangerous."

"Dangerous?" asked the orc. "What's so dangerous about books?"

"The books were only the beginning. The men would have been on television interviews, podcasts, videos, and all varieties of media. They would have been trending on social media.

The Mongolian Death Worm would have been the number one topic everywhere."

"Who cares?" the smaller orc said.

Dr. Hooey's face darkened. He slammed the table. "I care! You should care. All of us in the Society should care. Our mission is to study and protect cryptids and legendary monsters. We're supposed to keep them from being exploited and harmed. The very definition of a cryptid is a creature that has never been found. I couldn't allow that to happen. I couldn't allow the magnificent Mongolian Death Worm to be known to everyone. To become just another boring reptile.

"The creature has been the focus of my career." He sighed and wiped his eyes. "The center of my life. Their reputation is mine to protect. It's almost as if the worms are mine."

"Well, thanks to you, there are tons of worms burrowing beneath the beach," the smaller orc said. "Soon, one or more humans will capture specimens and turn them into 'boring reptiles.'"

"No! That will not happen! I've recruited the witch who works for us, and her boyfriend, to hunt them down."

"He's not my boyfriend," I muttered to myself.

"I gave her my pungi," the ickologist continued. "She should be able to coax them all to the surface and capture them so they can be euthanized."

"You would destroy the creatures you love?" asked the larger orc.

"Perhaps it was a misjudgment not to anticipate they would escape into the wild. But that unicorn is out of the barn. I must correct the mistake. We can't allow invasive species to run amok in environments where they don't belong. The worms belong in the Gobi Desert, not here. And certainly not in shallow books and online videos. I now have specimens for the Society to study and keep under control. That's all I desire."

The larger orc placed a printed document on the table in front of Dr. Hooey. "Please sign this confession."

The ickologist looked at the document as if it were an alien object. He appeared to be confused, as if he hadn't considered until now that he might be in legal jeopardy.

"I would need an attorney," he said just above a whisper.

"The Society will appoint one for you."

"I want to hire one of my own."

"That is not allowed," the justice agent replied. "This is a highly confidential matter that must remain within the jurisdiction of the Society. You will return to your cell, and an attorney will visit you."

Margaret Bullfinch pushed a button that made the wall panel slide back to its original position, covering the two-way mirror. "I believe we finally have this incident resolved."

"What about the human justice system?" I asked. "The victims have families who would want to see justice."

"I'm not at liberty to discuss this."

"What about Zora? Will you at least let her go?"

"She has already been released. She can resume her normal life, as long as she keeps her harpy identity hidden." Margaret's expression turned stern. "Your task is not to lecture us about justice, but to dispose of the loose worms."

"They must be disposed of?"

"Yes. We have plenty of live worms in captivity now. The ones infesting the beach will kill more innocent people unless they're removed. Do not feel guilty about killing them. In Florida, it is a necessity to capture and euthanize the invasive Burmese pythons. They have consumed over ninety percent of the mammals in the Everglades. Divers are encouraged to spearfish lionfish, which have inflicted similar damage to the ocean reef ecosystem. Go out there, get rid of the worms, and make us proud!"

"Count how many of them you eliminate," Mrs. Lupis said to me.

"For our records," Mr. Lopez added.

It was nearly a full moon, and the beach was silvery in the moonlight. The tide was low, making the beach wider than normal, affording plenty of room for worms to pop up.

And pop up they did. I played the pungi as Matt and I trudged from the southernmost point we thought worms would have spread toward the northernmost. As we marched, my pungi tunes began to sound more like New Orleans Dixieland jazz than Indian snake-charming music, but the tunes and the vibrations got the job done.

Worm after worm burrowed to the surface, drawn to the music, ravenous with thirst for the rainwater they believed was falling. Thanks to a spell I had devised, similar to the one that had tricked Asmodeus by disguising my blood, I blocked the scent of salt coming from the ocean. The worms rushed unawares toward what they thought was fresh water.

Playing the pungi, spreading my magic, I herded the worms right into the surf, where the saltwater quickly overwhelmed them. While Levings's pistol-packing neighbor had killed a worm with bullets, sending them en masse into the ocean was a much safer and more effective tactic than firing thousands of rounds on a public beach.

I tried to keep count of their numbers, as my handlers had requested. We dispatched at least forty, but it was difficult to count when the worms surfaced in groups.

We had begun our march after midnight, and thankfully, no people were on the beach. However, as we reached our northern goal, a solitary figure stood at the foot of the dune crossover stairs at a public beach. When we got closer, I recognized Detective Shortle.

"When I first heard your music, I thought you were crazy people," she said. "But then I saw what you were doing to the worms."

"Yeah. It's the best way to get rid of them." I waited for her to find an excuse to criticize us.

"Bless you," was what she said.

"Um, thank you."

"I'm one of the few officials who knows about the worm problem," Shortle said. "I've been trying to keep the public safe without creating a panic and destroying our tourism business. Are you actually going to solve our problem?"

"We're trying our best," I replied. "Don't be surprised if a stray worm shows up now and then. I can't guarantee we've taken care of them all. We're going to do another sweep of the beach in a couple of days, but if a worm is sighted, let me know. I'll take care of it."

"Are they drowning?"

"No. The salt in the water kills them almost instantly."

"I can't tell you how grateful I am."

"Please show your gratitude by keeping all of this secret," I begged. "After we're certain the worms are gone for good, please forget about them. Never breathe a word about them."

"Agreed."

"What's the status of your murder investigation?"

"Levings was killed, apparently by a worm that he kept as a pet," she replied. "We believe the fact that he had a worm makes it probable that he's the one who brought a worm, or worms, to Jellyfish Beach in the first place. We believe he bears responsibility for all the deaths from worms."

"I'm glad it's resolved."

"Me too," Matt said.

Matt and I left Shortle behind and continued patrolling north, clearing the beach and the bunkers of the golf course of death worms. Florida has sharks, alligators, venomous snakes, and plenty of other critters that could kill you. We didn't need Mongolian death worms. And hopefully, from this point forward, you'd have to go to the Gobi Desert to find one. If you brought a pungi with you, that is.

Matt and I parted just before dawn in the beach parking lot. I leaned forward, wanting a lingering kiss of moderate heat, just spicy enough to show there was passion between us, but not enough to complicate my life just yet.

Instead, Matt pulled away after a quick peck on the lips.

"I should tell you I have a date tomorrow night," he said. "Nothing serious."

"Date? You mean, with a woman?"

"Officer Bird and I are meeting for coffee."

My concern surprised me. "Isn't that a conflict of interest—

a reporter who covers crime dating a cop? One who's like half his age?"

"We're not dating. It's just a friendly get-together between colleagues. You know, to improve relations with a source. I'm only telling you in case someone sees Susan and me together and misinterprets it."

"Her name is Susan? I thought it was just Officer Bird."

He chuckled. "Don't act so affronted. I'll tell you all about it afterwards."

Affronted? Me, affronted?

When I got home, I gave Tony and the cats an early breakfast and left a voicemail with Luisa that I would come in late for work at the botanica after a much-needed nap. Before I put the phone down, I noticed an earlier voicemail was there for me.

"There's a special meeting of my coven tomorrow evening at seven," Ruth said. "You'd better be there, dearie, or I shall be forced to kill you." She cackled diabolically like the Wicked Witch of the West.

If it's not one thing, it's another, in this life of mine. I resolved to stop fretting about Matt's "date." I was the one who had been avoiding commitment, so I had to live with the consequences. Still, this development was bothering me more than I expected, but I resolved to push it from my mind. At least for tonight.

I also decided to blow off the meeting with Ruth and crawled into bed with two warm cats. Life would be so good if only the evil creatures would leave me alone. I had enough merely weird creatures to keep me busy.

The pitter-patter of reptilian feet on hardwood floors told me that one of these weird creatures had entered my room.

"Mind if I sleep in here?" Tony asked. "I'm having nightmares about worms."

"Yeah. Go ahead."

My cats hissed in disagreement with my decision. But before long, my four-legged family members—both warm- and cold-blooded—fell into contented sleep.

PLEASE LEAVE A REVIEW

Dear reader, thank you in advance:
Please give my book a better chance.
Success and sales depend on you,
So kindly post a book review.

WHAT'S NEXT

Coming soon, Book 8 of Monsters of Jellyfish Beach: *Haint Misbehavin'*. More details to come.

Sign up for my newsletter

Get a free novella when you join my occasional newsletter filled with updates on new releases, special deals, and amusing content. All you have to do is visit wardparker.com

ACKNOWLEDGMENTS

I wish to thank my loyal readers, who give me a reason to write more every day. I'm especially grateful to my editors and proofreaders for their eagle eyes. To my A Team (you know who you are), thanks for reading and reviewing my ARCs, as well as providing good suggestions. And to my wife, Martha, thank you for your graphic design brilliance as well as your love and moral support.

ABOUT THE AUTHOR

Ward is the author of the Memory Guild midlife paranormal mystery thrillers and its urban fantasy sequel series, The Goddess's Daughter, as well as the Freaky Florida series, set in the same world as Monsters of Jellyfish Beach, with Missy, Matt, Agnes, and many other familiar characters.

Ward lives in Florida with his wife, several cats, and a demon who wishes to remain anonymous.

Connect with him on social media: Bluesky, Facebook (wardparkerauthor), BookBub, Goodreads, and Pinterest, or check out his books at wardparker.com.

PARANORMAL BOOKS BY WARD PARKER

Freaky Florida Humorous Paranormal Novels

Snowbirds of Prey

Invasive Species

Fate Is a Witch

Gnome Coming

Going Batty

Dirty Old Manatee

Gazillions of Reptilians

Hangry as Hell (novella)

Books 1-3 Box Set

The Memory Guild Midlife Paranormal Mystery Thrillers

A Magic Touch (also available in audio)

The Psychic Touch (also available in audio)

A Wicked Touch (also available in audio)

A Haunting Touch

The Wizard's Touch

A Witchy Touch

A Faerie's Touch

The Goddess's Touch

The Vampire's Touch

An Angel's Touch

A Ghostly Touch (novella)

Books 1-3 Box Set (also available in audio)

Complete Series, Books 1-10, Box Set

The Goddess's Daughter Urban Fantasy Trilogy

(Sequel to the Memory Guild Series.)

Of Envy and Empaths

Of Fear and Fae

Of Vampires and Valor

Monsters of Jellyfish Beach Paranormal Mystery Adventures

The Golden Ghouls

Fiends With Benefits

Get Ogre Yourself
My Funny Frankenstein
Werewolf Art Thou?
In Sprite of Herself
Worms of Endearment

www.ingramcontent.com/pod-product-compliance
Lightning Source LLC
LaVergne TN
LVHW091121080826
845145LV00008B/1999

* 9 7 8 1 9 5 7 1 5 8 2 6 6 *